PRAISE FOR
WHEN THERE'S NOWHERE ELSE TO RUN

'Middleton moves between hilarious and affecting in the space of a sentence, and some of these stories brought me to tears.'
—*Adelaide Advertiser*

'An exquisite short story collection.' —Booktopia

'Shows great deftness in portraying place and landscape and effective characterisation of people living under pressure . . . Middleton's passion for trying to write the truth simply, without excess or floridness, has served him well in this collection.'
—*Canberra Times*

'In *When There's Nowhere Else to Run,* Murray Middleton is not afraid to show us his heart.' —*The Saturday Paper*

'His collection, which won this year's *The Australian*/Vogel's Literary Award, is harrowing and beautiful, charting lives that are broken and disconnected, disrupted and in pain . . . important Australian debut by a major new talent.' —*Weekend Australian*

'Vivid and compelling.' —Jenny Barry, BooksPlus

Murray Middleton was born with fractured hips in 1983. He spent the first three months of his life in plaster and has broken most bones since. He won *The Age* Short Story Award in 2010 with 'The Fields of Early Sorrow'. *When There's Nowhere Else to Run* is his first published collection of short stories. He currently lives in Melbourne and won't publish a second collection of stories until the Saints win a second premiership.

WHEN THERE'S NOWHERE ELSE TO RUN

MURRAY MIDDLETON

ALLEN&UNWIN

SYDNEY · MELBOURNE · AUCKLAND · LONDON

The story 'The Fields of Early Sorrow' has been published previously and revised for this
edition. It won *The Age* Short Story Award in 2010 and was published in *The Age* and
the *Sydney Morning Herald* on 8 January 2011. This story was also published in *Award
Winning Australian Writing 2011*.

Allen & Unwin
83 Alexander Street
Crows Nest NSW 2065
Australia
Phone: (61 2) 8425 0100
Email: info@allenandunwin.com
Web: www.allenandunwin.com

Cataloguing-in-Publication details are available
from the National Library of Australia
www.trove.nla.gov.au

ISBN 978 1 76029 258 4

Typeset in Fairfield LT Std by Bookhouse, Sydney
Printed and bound in Australia by Griffin Press

10 9 8 7 6 5 4 3

For L.D. and my family

CONTENTS

CONTENTS

OPEN
MISÈRE

I'm not sure how Mum and Dad planned on spending their long-service leave. Maybe planting jonquils, solving cryptic crosswords and firing chestnuts at the cockatoo that Dad called Kasparov. Maybe they wanted to see Europe for the first time, although they would've had to see it in winter because of the footy. Either way, I bet they didn't plan on spending it with our old neighbour, Raymond, lying on a foldout bed in the study.

Raymond lived around the corner from us in Tecoma when I was little. That was before he bought ten acres just outside Marysville. I couldn't remember much about him. The main thing that stuck in my mind was that he had a sweet tooth. Mum used to wonder how he slept at night with all that sugar swimming through his veins. But at least he slept back then.

When Raymond came to visit, Mum and Dad told me not to mention the fires. At first it was easy enough. He didn't seem to be in the mood for talking. I hadn't thought much about the fires. Before his visit, nothing in my life had changed as a result of them. Growing up in the hills, I'd got used to hearing the CFA siren every summer. We always took it as a chance to visit Granddad in the city. If there was time, Mum and Dad would fill the gutters with water and hose down the roof, but there was never any talk of staying home to fight.

What I remember best about the Black Saturday fires is the newsreader in Kinglake who was live on air when he found out that his friend—the previous anchor—had passed away. I can't remember the newsreader's name. The realisation of what had happened seemed to come across his face all at once. His cheeks went very pale. It got me thinking that seeing death in the faces of the living might be scarier than seeing an open casket.

■

Our lives were all about rituals after Raymond came to visit. We played a game of Five Hundred every afternoon. Mum said that for the time being I wasn't allowed to visit friends' houses after school. The games lasted anywhere between half an hour and two hours, depending on how stubborn Dad was feeling. Raymond didn't seem to have much interest in playing. He'd usually sit there nursing a packet of scorched almonds. Sometimes when it was his turn to bid he'd just stare into space, like he'd forgotten where he was, until Dad got his attention. Then he'd pass. He even passed when he had the joker. It could get frustrating when I was Raymond's partner, having to do all the work, but I knew I wasn't allowed to complain.

Dad tried to get him back into the footy. He told me that Raymond used to play in the Yarra Valley League over twenty years ago. Apparently he was a decent full-back. I couldn't see it. We'd all watch the Demons game on TV every weekend. They'd had some high draft picks in the last few years and Dad was sure it wouldn't be long until they were on the way back up again. Mum wasn't quite as convinced. Raymond never barracked. I often caught him staring out the window with the same blank look that he wore while we were playing cards.

Between cards and dinner, Mum and Dad would take Raymond for a walk in the forest near Grants Picnic Ground. They said it was good for him to leave the house every day. Dad bought him a pair of gumboots from Bunnings because the tracks got muddy in winter. I joined them once or twice at the beginning and I noticed that Mum and Dad were steering clear of the more popular walking tracks.

Before dinner every night one of us had to tell a joke. I'm pretty sure it was Dad's idea. It was usually a bad joke, too. When it was my turn, I stole puns from the net because that's what seemed to make Mum and Dad happy. They always had a good chuckle, even when the jokes didn't entirely work out. Dad laughed differently, though. It came more out of his nose. At times it really got on my nerves and I wanted to tell him to laugh normally.

For all the effort we made, what Raymond seemed to like most of all was sitting out on the porch in the morning, eating his raisin toast. I didn't mind him sitting out there as much as Mum and Dad. They didn't want him spending too much time alone, but since he was always the first person up, there wasn't really anything they could do about it. The raisin toast left a sweet, burnt sultana smell throughout the house while I was getting ready for school. When I got home Raymond was usually still sitting out there on the bench that Dad had painted red and blue, watching the mist drift over the valley.

■

I'd met Courtney at a party a few months before Raymond came to visit. The Mater Christi girls were there, which meant we all put our hands in our pockets more and talked about sport less. Courtney was always distracting me from studying for my mid-year exams. She didn't seem to care about hers. She came round three afternoons a week (she worked the register at Woolworths on Thursday and Friday). Mum and Dad didn't mind her staying over on weekends. They said it was better than us making up stories.

We tried to teach Courtney how to play Five Hundred by practising some open hands while Raymond was sitting out on the porch. She understood the bidding, but she had a fair bit of trouble remembering how the bowers worked. She was much better when the bid was no trumps. Mum always asked Courtney to score when we were playing with Raymond to help her get a feel for the game. I could tell no one liked it when she started doodling on the notepad, and I hoped it didn't mean she was bored.

I don't think I'll ever forget what went on while the adults were out walking in the forest. Whenever Courtney threw her school dress on my bedroom carpet, it made me feel proud in a silent way, like I had something over most of the boys at school. For a number of reasons I'd always assumed that nothing like that would ever happen to me. I said Courtney's name out loud a lot, which was never something I planned on doing. I tried really hard not to say it. But she didn't mind, even though she never said my name out loud.

Courtney didn't like the way that Raymond sat there on the porch when she was walking up the driveway in the afternoon. She thought he was waiting for her. We had a few spats about him. She was much better at arguing than me. Afterwards I could always think of all the things that I should have said in the heat of the argument. Courtney never left much unsaid.

We were in bed one time, a week or two after Raymond had come to visit, and she asked me how long he was going to be staying with us. She was lying on her stomach, chopping bud on my psychology textbook. We usually had about an hour when the adults were out walking. It didn't stop me feeling anxious about them coming home early.

'I've got no idea how long he'll be here,' I said, stroking her hair. 'Mum and Dad haven't said much about it.'

'Does he pay for any of the food he's eating?'

'I'm not really sure.'

Raymond did seem to have an endless supply of scorched almonds, but I'd never stopped to think about whether he paid for them.

'On my way out yesterday I caught him in the kitchen with his fingers in the peanut butter,' said Courtney. She laughed. 'He was just sort of pawing it into his mouth. It was really weird. I didn't know what to do, so I just kind of left. There was peanut butter all over his chin.' She put down the scissors and started mixing tobacco with the bud.

'I can't imagine him doing that,' I said.

'Well, that's what he did.' She reached into her handbag and grabbed the cigarette papers.

'I guess I'll be avoiding the peanut butter then,' I said.

Courtney grinned as she started packing the paper. She was the first person who ever made me feel like I might be funny.

■

I sometimes heard Mum and Dad talking about Raymond in their bedroom at night. They never argued. I could tell they were talking about him because their conversations were in a different pitch than usual. It was a strange thing. When I heard them talking, I realised how little trouble I must have given them over the years.

I couldn't say whether Raymond overheard their conversations from the study or, if he did, whether he cared. I figured that our aim was to help him feel normal again. I had no idea what constituted 'normal'. Before I met Courtney, I thought that I was painfully normal. I wondered whether Raymond had been normal before he moved to Marysville, with all that sugar swimming through his veins. All I concluded was that once the state was lost, whatever it was, it probably became impossible to find again.

Mum and Dad did their best to keep Raymond away from the papers in case something about the royal commission popped up. They didn't mind me leaving the sports section on the table. Mum tried to get him interested in doing the cryptic crossword, but the clues never seemed to mean anything to him. Before Raymond came to visit, Mum and Dad used to solve all three crosswords every night after dinner. They even solved the crosswords when there were piles of essays all over the house, waiting to be marked. Courtney thought it was a lame way for them to spend their time. She made me promise that we'd never be so pathetic when we were old.

At dinner Dad would tell us all about his ongoing battles with Kasparov the cockatoo. No one was really listening. Over the Easter holidays he'd made a slingshot by rigging a heavy rubber band over a coathanger. I don't know what he would have done without Kasparov. He finally convinced Raymond to join him in the yard one afternoon. Even though Raymond took a carton of chestnuts out with him, he refused to have a turn on the slingshot.

When Mum and Dad visited the McCartneys in Sassafras— which they had done every Sunday since their daughter Fay moved interstate—they insisted that Raymond went with them. I was relieved because I didn't want to be alone with him. It was the only good run I ever got at studying. I pictured him brooding over a glass of cola on the patio at the McCartneys' house, maybe rubbing their labrador's belly while the others talked about films and the footy, missing his raisin toast.

There were times when Raymond took some coaxing to leave the house. It was usually just after we'd finished playing cards. He'd say he was feeling sleepy or he didn't need the exercise. He was never rude about it. Mum was always the one to reason with him. Those were the only times I resented him, especially when Courtney was over. His excuses made me feel angry in a way I never had before. We all knew he was eventually going to put on his gumboots. Courtney would just smile while Mum was talking Raymond into it, like she knew what was going on inside me and that was the funniest part.

■

We were stumbling up the driveway in the dark, trying to avoid Dad's jonquils, when I noticed that the kitchen light was still on. It was hours after Mum and Dad usually went to bed. I got Courtney to brush the twigs off the back of my hoodie. Mum, Dad and Raymond were sitting in the dining room, listening to terrible folk music. There were two empty wine bottles on the table and they were working on a third. Raymond was resting his purple cheek on his hand. Mum had hold of his other hand.

'How was the party?' asked Mum.

'Good,' I said, trying to sound normal. 'It was more of a gathering.'

'Any fatalities?' asked Dad.

Courtney pressed her mouth against my shoulder to stop herself from laughing.

'How was your night?' I asked. I had no idea who I was addressing the question to.

'We had a quiet night in,' said Mum. She patted Raymond's arm. The flesh on his cheeks seemed to be softening. It was more unnerving than watching him stare into space.

'Well, goodnight,' I said.

Courtney let out a loud laugh when we were halfway down the corridor, so I cupped my hand over her mouth.

■

I was sitting out on the porch at two o'clock in the morning because I was having trouble sleeping. My Australian history exam was first thing in the morning. Even though I was under-prepared, I figured I'd clean up on the essay. It was close to freezing. I was fumbling underneath the bench in my usual hiding place when Raymond appeared. He asked if I minded the intrusion and I said that I didn't. His joints clicked when he sat next to me.

'I swore I'd never resent the cold again,' he said.

I didn't know what to say to that. We sat there in silence, staring out over the dark valley. My breath was making small clouds. Every so often I'd hear a car zooming through the forest. I used to have nightmares about a grey car tumbling off the road in the forest and rolling down the valley, somehow missing all the mountain ash trees, never stopping. But since I'd started smoking, I'd stopped having dreams.

'Do you remember much about it?' he asked.

'About what?'

'The day.'

'Black Saturday?' The words sounded heavy.

Raymond nodded.

'We went to visit Granddad to get away from the fires. I think we stayed inside most of the day. It was really windy. The sky was a funny colour.' I realised I'd put my foot in it. 'Not funny . . .'

'It's okay,' said Raymond, still looking out over the valley. 'I know what you mean.'

'Mum and Dad were pretty upset when we watched the news.'

The cypresses along the driveway were beginning to sway.

'Did she get you into that stuff?' asked Raymond.

'Sorry?'

He waved his hand. 'I don't care. It's nice to watch you two.'

I decided never to tell Courtney what he'd just said.

'I bet you make all kinds of promises to each other.'

'Not that many,' I said, laughing a little.

He kept on staring into the darkness like he expected something to be out there. The skin on his cheeks looked loose enough to stitch and fold into curtains.

'Why don't you tell me about one?' he said.

'I don't know, they're all pretty boring.'

'Boring's fine,' he said, glancing under the bench. 'You might as well light it.'

I reached down and found the half-smoked joint. I lit it and offered it to Raymond.

'No thanks,' he said. 'Go on.'

I inhaled and tried to think of a promise.

'Last week, while you guys were out walking in the forest, we made a pact that in twenty years' time, no matter what, we're going to meet at Burke's Lookout on our anniversary. Courtney's going to bring Frosty Fruits.'

'Frosty Fruits,' said Raymond, raising his heavy cheeks and shaking his head. 'Won't they melt?'

'She said she's going to bring an esky.'

It took Raymond several minutes to get over the idea of Courtney bringing Frosty Fruits along. I couldn't see how it was that funny and I was worried he might wake Mum and Dad.

■

The next afternoon Raymond opened the bidding with a call of six clubs. Mum and I bumped the call up to eight diamonds, but then Raymond bid open misère. I'd never seen an open misère bid and I had to explain to Courtney what it meant. 'Bring it home, Ray!' yelled Dad, laying his cards face down on the table and flashing his fillings at Mum. I could feel Courtney's hand working its way up my thigh. Raymond picked up the kitty and started complaining that it'd given him nothing. It was nice to hear him complaining.

BIG
BUFFALO

Jennifer Pfeiffer was always giving me instructions such as, 'Stay with me, Henry, don't lose it!' Sometimes she told me off. 'No, no, you're doing it all wrong today. Not yet!' I always tried to comply. I feared that if I didn't, she might find someone else to give instructions to and they might be better at following them than me. My favourite part was when she closed her eyes, arched her spine and her breathing grew heavy. I knew I was doing everything just right. Her orgasm would come in small spurts at first, followed by an almighty surge. It felt like everything that I had ever wanted in this world.

Apart from the first time, it always took place at the Ramada Inn on Royal Parade (I believe the motel has since changed names). I chose it because I liked the surrounding parklands.

After I had showered and returned the key to reception, I would often sit on a bench overlooking the zoo to have a good think about what I was up to. I got to thinking about what a motel room actually meant to a man. To me it meant secrecy, haste, pleasure, guilt and many other ill-fated words. But bringing to mind those words was never enough to stop me showing up the next week.

We met in the same room every Sunday morning. I worked full time at David Kesselbach Financial Planning. My wife Robyn worked at Zeneli Flowers on weekends. Jennifer ran a stall at the Rose Street Artists' Market every Saturday and spent most of the week sewing, picking up fabrics and making jewellery. I wasn't interested in exploiting half-hour gaps in our respective schedules. That approach is for men in European films.

One Sunday in August, Robyn woke with a fever and called in sick to work, although I tried to convince her otherwise. A few minutes later I closed the ensuite door, switched on the fan and called Jennifer to cancel. She said it was okay. Throughout the following week I was constantly distracted at work by thoughts of her naked form. Nothing like that had ever happened to me before. It wasn't enough for her to haunt my imagination. I needed flesh on flesh. By Saturday night I had come down with the fever, but it didn't stop me sneaking off to the motel the next morning.

I always experienced a range of emotions on my walk to the Ramada Inn. I enjoyed the vast nature strips, the empty elm trees, the crunch of the brown leaves, and the dew that often blanketed the parklands in the morning. I wasn't sure how I could commit such unpleasantness in the face of such beauty. I had always assumed that I would lead a life devoid of unpleasantness. It was astounding how simple it had been to shatter my assumption.

I often passed a group of white-haired men playing bocce in the heart of Princes Park. They tended to address each other in an animated fashion. It was difficult to tell whether they were being jovial or not. Over the course of the winter, one of the men took to acknowledging me. We never exchanged words, but he would nod or tilt the brim of his felt hat. Somehow it affirmed that an act was taking place.

The only other person who was complicit in my deceit was the motel attendant, a plump woman called Alicia. She spoke to me in a painfully dignified manner. 'We hope you have a nice stay.' I sometimes felt tempted to offer her an explanation as I was handing over the money. But there was no point, since she had probably seen hundreds of people who were up to the same trick as me.

The whole thing started while my son Paul was on a six-month student exchange in France. His host family lived in a small port town called Dinan. I was adamant that when he returned in the summer, I would stop seeing Jennifer. I loved Paul. I loved the fact that he had asked us to call him once a week while he was away, instead of every second night (which was what Robyn had proposed). I rarely considered that I might love Jennifer Pfeiffer, or that she might love me.

◼

We had driven Paul to the airport on a drizzly Friday night. There was a thunderstorm forecast, but it looked like it might be holding off. I practised some French phrases with him in the front seat. *'Je voudrais un croissant, s'il vous plaît.'* Robyn started weeping when we reached the Tullamarine exit on the Ring Road.

She barely slept that night. When I awoke the next morning, she had already left for work. There was a note on the kitchen bench:

> Morning,
> Paul called from the terminal in Shanghai, no major
> dramas. Can you pick up a wholemeal loaf from Babka
> when you get the chance? It's under your name.
> Love,
> Robyn

As I studied my wife's neat handwriting, it occurred to me that my Saturday and Sunday mornings were no longer confined to the errands of junior sport.

I decided to walk to the bakery. The main café strip of Fitzroy was already in full swing. Bicycles were chained to street signs. Students with fluffy beards lingered at the windows of bookshops. I had to wait in a long line at Babka. Rosy-cheeked waitresses weaved between cramped tables, serving coffees, pastries and cakes. A young woman with dreadlocks was writing a note on a serviette by the window. It was strange to think that there was even a loaf on the premises with my name written on it.

On my way home I was stopped by a man who was dressed in leather from head to toe. There was a studded collar around his neck. It made me wonder about his parents. He said something to me in a gruff voice. I reached into my pocket, but he waved the gesture away. He handed me a leaflet for the Rose Street Artists' Market before turning his attention to a group of young women who were approaching.

I found the market in a side street wedged between old brick warehouses and new apartment blocks. Despite working within a two-kilometre radius for the past sixteen years, I hadn't been aware of its existence. I walked a circuit of the courtyard, pausing occasionally to feign interest in a hand-bound book or an environmentally sustainable greeting card. At the rear of the site was a garage with small theatre lights suspended along the ceiling. One of the stalls inside displayed a sea of rings that had been made out of recycled cutlery. I stopped at a secluded stall that was bordered by trestle tables, and browsed through a rack of hemp t-shirts.

'Can I help you?' asked an attractive middle-aged woman who was sitting in the centre of the stall. She was wearing an emerald bow ring on her left ring finger.

'I'm just looking,' I said.

'That's no fun.' She frowned in a way that made me want to tell her not to frown. 'Why don't you try one on?' she said.

I laid the wholemeal loaf on a trestle table and pulled one of the t-shirts over my woollen jumper. It was black with an image of a red buffalo. 'Does this suit me?'

'I wouldn't know.'

I laughed, even though I couldn't tell if it was a joke or not. There were dozens more of the emerald bow rings on display in a small wicker basket.

'Alright then,' I said. 'I'll take it.'

I handed her a fifty-dollar note and she rummaged in a fluorescent orange pouch that was clipped around her waist.

'How long have you had a stall here?' I asked.

'Almost a year now,' she said, sounding enthusiastic. 'I moved down from Sydney last winter. I'm here every Saturday.'

She handed me the change. I decided not to ask if she had a plastic bag.

'And what does Big Buffalo do for a living?' she asked.

'I'm a financial planner.'

She nodded and made a funny nasal noise. 'Is that like being an accountant?'

'There's a bit of an overlap. I always say to clients, we plan for the future whereas accountants make the past add up.'

'So you make people rich.'

'That's not the main idea. It's more about providing sound financial advice and finding the best way to transfer assets to our clients' beneficiaries.'

She was nodding and making the noise again.

'It probably sounds a bit dry to you,' I said.

'Nope, sounds interesting. Maybe you can wear your new shirt to work on Monday.'

'Yes, maybe.'

(To this day I haven't worn the t-shirt again, but I haven't thrown it out.)

'My finances are in a bit of a mess at the moment,' she said. 'I hope I don't end up in jail.'

'I'm sure it's not that serious,' I said, laughing.

The next Saturday I volunteered to buy a wholemeal loaf from Babka.

■

When I emerged from the reception block, I noticed that Jennifer's red Daihatsu wasn't in the car park. She was always the first to arrive. For several minutes I leant against the handrail outside our room, waiting for her. It was a brisk spring morning. There had been heavy rain overnight. I eventually realised that the puddle I was staring at was in the space where Jennifer usually parked. I imagined her visiting a used-car dealership in the western suburbs and shaking hands with a fleshy, thin-haired man inside the showroom. I imagined them taking the hatchback for a test drive and his thoughts slithering from the prospective sale to what was beneath her summer dress.

I opened the door and left it unlocked, unsure how I was going to pass the time until she got there. There was a small concrete balcony off the room that had a chair, a table and an ashtray. I sat down on the chair and admired the quiet avenue that ran between the motel and the tennis courts. Even though the clay was still damp, two boys were playing. Over the course of their match, the sun came out, creating long shadows from the cypresses behind the courts. As the boys were sweeping the clay and brushing the lines, I realised that I'd been watching them for almost an hour and that Jennifer mightn't be coming.

I returned to the room and lay in the centre of the bed. It was too firm for my liking. I had never actually slept at the Ramada Inn, so I closed my eyes. The main indicator of time elapsing was the regular blaring of train horns along the Upfield line. I counted six blasts. It began to feel as though an injustice was taking place. From the outset I had been certain that I would be the one to end it. I had even practised in my head what I was going to say. Every time I heard the sound of tyres choking in the car park, I felt a pinch of excitement. I would stare at the door handle and will it to revolve. When it didn't oblige within thirty seconds, the frustration would return.

I wondered what Paul was up to. He never gave much away over the phone. I calculated that it was around three o'clock in the morning in France. Hopefully he was in bed. I remembered a joke that he had told Robyn and me one evening, many years earlier, after he had returned home from school camp. Did you hear about the dyslexic atheist who was suffering from insomnia? He lay awake all night wondering if there was a Dog. I was still smiling when Jennifer finally walked in.

'What's so funny?' she asked.

'It doesn't matter.'

'Sorry I'm late, Henry.'

I felt a strong sensation inside my chest. It was difficult to gauge whether it was affection or relief. 'I was beginning to think you weren't coming.'

'I already said I'm sorry.'

'I know, but you've wasted my whole morning.'

I was disappointed when she didn't react to the firmness in my tone.

'How did it make you feel when you thought I wasn't coming?'

She was wearing her hair in a high ponytail. Her eyebrows looked thinner than they had the previous Sunday. Her eyes—which sometimes took on a hazel shade when the curtains were open—looked dark and heavy.

'I felt unwanted.'

She sighed. 'We all feel unwanted, Henry.'

'No, it was more than that. I felt terrible for wanting something so harmful to the people I love.'

Jennifer removed her suede jacket, but lingered beside the bed. I hoped that she was going to come to me. After about a minute I reached for her hand and started stroking the loose skin between her thumb and her forefinger. She collapsed to the bed and I raised my arm, allowing her head to nestle in the hollow between my collarbone and the ball of my shoulder. Her hair smelt like incense (she once told me that her favourite scent was called Nag Champa). I extended my hand to her stomach and felt it rise and fall.

I felt compelled to issue a statement of affection for her. The problem with such statements is that they can't be retracted once they escape your lips. And then they might exist as ransom. Once or twice—through acts of pleasure—Jennifer had almost induced false admissions of love from me.

'I don't want you to feel terrible,' she said. 'That's the last thing I want you to feel.'

She slowly guided my hand along her ribcage. She had smaller, more pliant breasts than Robyn. I liked them a great deal. I had often put them in my mouth, which was something that I hadn't done with any other woman.

■

I experienced a surge of remorse while Jennifer was in the bathroom. She never flushed after doing a number one. I figured it was a habit she had probably picked up while studying costume design at NIDA. The sight of the yellow liquid and the toilet paper plastered to the side of the bowl repulsed me. It meant I had to flush both before I went and afterwards, which defeated the purpose of her having left it there. Robyn always flushed, no matter what. Jennifer returned to the bed and settled underneath the covers. I kept my hands to myself.

'Just out of interest,' she said, 'what happens when your son comes back?'

Tennis balls were being slugged from end to end outside.

'Did you hear me, Henry?'

I nodded.

'You haven't even told me his name.' She started sobbing. It was the first time she had cried in my presence.

'His name's Paul,' I said. 'Paul Belanger.'

Jennifer's sobbing eventually softened into a series of faint coughs. I reached for the bedside table, but realised there wasn't a tissue box. I had the wrong bedroom.

'What's he like?'

23

'Who, Paul?' I asked, knowing full well whom she meant.

She nodded and sniffled.

'He's a nice, normal kid, very polite, much more polite than his father.'

'I want to know more than that, please.'

My right hand had come to rest on Jennifer's stomach. I couldn't remember the thought that had preceded the action.

'He's very studious. His favourite subjects at school are legal studies and maths methods. I'm sure his French is great now, too. The teachers always have nice things to say about him at parent–teacher nights. He doesn't like me interfering with his studies, or his personal life, for that matter.' I stopped, aware that I was waffling. 'I'm not sure if this is what you want. Am I doing alright here?'

'You're doing fine, keep going.'

'He's very particular about his hair. It might be because there are girls in his life. If there are, he certainly doesn't talk to me about them. I think he'd be a great catch, but I'm not the most objective person on the subject. It doesn't matter anyway. He's still young; young enough to make mistakes, and young enough for those mistakes to be forgiven.'

I lowered my hand.

'Please don't,' she said. 'Just keep telling me about him.'

'I'm not sure what else there is. He has good friends. He's

known most of them since he was in primary school. They're at ease with each other. It's really nice to watch, actually. Since Paul's been overseas, I've missed seeing his friends. I'm only talking about five minutes here and there around the house, or in the car on the way to tennis, but it all adds up. Sometimes I see kids on drugs near the flats and I remember how lucky I am. I always try to be thankful.'

I had that strange feeling I sometimes got at the reception desk when I was paying Alicia for the room.

'You might make certain assumptions about me,' I said, 'but this is all new to me.'

'I know,' she said. Her stomach was rumbling. 'What does he want to do when he's older?'

'The last time I checked, he wanted to study law. I've suggested insolvency law, but I think he's got bigger fish to fry, which is fine. He'll need to maintain his grades if he wants to get in to Melbourne Uni. It's very competitive. I took him to the open day last year so he could get a feel for the campus.'

'You must really love him.'

'Of course I do.' I ran my fingers along Jennifer's ribcage.

'That tickles,' she said flatly.

It was strange, because in my experience people either smiled or grimaced when something tickled.

'So what happens when Paul comes home?' she asked.

'Everything goes back to normal.'

By this time on a Sunday we would normally have done it three times.

'This could be normal,' said Jennifer.

'No it couldn't.'

'Why not?'

'You know why.'

'I want to hear you say it.'

I half expected her to start sobbing again, but she remained disconcertingly quiet. I already knew that I would miss her instructions.

'Because there'd be too many complications,' I said.

In light of the recent exchange of words, I wondered whether I should remove my hand from her ribcage. I didn't. We lay in silence and I started counting the train horns again.

■

The last time I saw Jennifer Pfeiffer was in the menswear section of Myer. It was a year and a half after we had stopped seeing each other. I was with Paul. He'd had a growth spurt and was now almost an inch taller than me. We were doing a last-minute shop for warm clothes before he moved to the Deakin campus on the outskirts of Warrnambool.

'Henry!' she called out, approaching us. 'I thought that was you.'

She was holding a three-pack of business socks. I introduced her to Paul and she shook his hand.

'Little Buffalo,' said Jennifer, placing her hand on Paul's forearm.

'Who?' he asked.

'You've got your father's eyes.' She continued to examine his features. I had no idea whether he suspected anything.

'Do you still have a stall at the market?' I asked.

'You bet,' she said. 'I'm working Sundays now, too. Everything's great.' She smiled in a way I had never seen her smile. 'And how's the financial-planning business going?' she asked.

'We're still very busy.'

'I'm an old client of your father's,' she said, glancing at Paul.

It occurred to me that I never did find out whether her finances were in a mess.

'Well, we'd better get back to it,' I said. 'Best of luck with the stall.'

In bed that night I got to thinking about a frosty morning that Jennifer and I had spent at the Ramada Inn. I couldn't even see the tennis courts out the window because of the condensation. She was kneeling on top of me. Her eyes looked like dark marbles. It was warm inside her. It felt like a safe place to spend the winter. She told me to leave it in. No thrusting, nothing. I asked her for how long, and she said, 'As long as it takes.' She closed her eyes, arched her spine and her breathing slowly grew heavier.

As I peeled back the covers and found my way to the bathroom in the dark, I hoped that Paul would never need to feel anything like it.

MAINSTREAM

'Mum, something funny is happening to my ears,' said Harrison, leaning back in his seat, gripping the armrests and tilting his head upwards. It was his first time on an aeroplane. I used to chew gum to help with the take-off, but I hadn't packed any because he didn't like the texture.

'If you swallow your saliva it helps your ears go pop,' I said.

'Pop!' he said.

He held the pose, trying to aid the aircraft in its ascent over the brown hills of Adelaide.

'Why don't you try to find Grandma's house?' I said, pointing out the window.

'Pop!'

The seatbelt sign above us was soon switched off. Harrison spent the next twenty minutes staring at the fluorescent cigarette next to it. I eventually managed to distract him by removing *Peter Pan* from my backpack. He slowly traced his finger over the illustrations, only turning each page when he had absorbed every last detail on it. Halfway through the flight one of the flight attendants—a doll in her mid-twenties with her hair coiled in a slick bun—asked if Harrison wanted to visit the cockpit.

'Go on,' I said. 'You'll love it.'

I doubted that he could cause an aeroplane crash, even though he had just been expelled from school. I unbuckled his seatbelt and he crawled from the window seat, over my lap, and dropped into the aisle with a thud. I could sense people staring.

'Would you like to come too?' asked the flight attendant, smiling at me condescendingly.

'No thanks, I'm fine here.'

Harrison ignored the flight attendant's outstretched hand, but followed her along the aisle. I moved to the window seat and stared at the bed of white clouds below. I had forgotten how peaceful it felt to fly above them. I used to love reading on aeroplanes, but *Peter Pan* was the only book I'd packed.

I remembered my first flight, when I was nineteen. It was only fourteen years ago, but it felt like a different lifetime. I was flying to Vanuatu with my friend Melissa Tang. As the plane was approaching New Caledonia, I caught sight of the coral reefs out the window. They looked like the lungs of the turquoise ocean. It had struck me that there were infinite tiers of beauty beyond our mainland, waiting to be peeled back over the course of a human life.

Melissa and I slept with nine men between us in the week we spent at Le Meridien resort. I could only remember one of the men's names. John. He was twenty years older than me and he was a business development manager with one of the major insurance companies in Melbourne. He didn't think there was any shame in having fun on a holiday. As I was undoing my bra, I asked him to take his wedding ring off and put it on the bedside table.

I hadn't seen Melissa in six years, but we still sent each other Christmas cards. She'd moved to Sydney to work for the Department of Infrastructure and Transport. The last Christmas card had a photo of her and her fiancé, Vincent, at a charity golf day. He looked tall, outgoing and much younger than her. It wasn't difficult to imagine them meeting at a bar overlooking the harbour and exchanging phone numbers. They had just moved into a rented North Shore apartment. In the card Melissa had written that I was welcome to visit any time. She didn't mention Harrison.

■

The minibus driver was standing outside the airport terminal, continually checking his watch. He insisted on putting our 'luggage' in the boot, even though I was only carrying a back-pack. Harrison couldn't stop staring at the driver's hideous red goatee.

'Where you headed?' he asked, nestling the backpack between suitcases.

'Drive us anywhere,' I said.

He grimaced. 'What do you mean?'

'Do you know a cheap place we can stay tonight?'

'There might be some vacancies at the YMCA. It's tough to know at this hour.'

'Great, take us there.'

He ushered us into the minibus. There were elderly people sitting in the two front rows. He spent the next few minutes answering questions from them.

'My guess is we'll make it into the city in fifteen minutes,' he said in a patronisingly loud voice. 'Maybe fourteen minutes if we get all the green lights.'

We drove past the car dealerships, the service stations and the bright lights of McDonald's before crossing the Swan River. The driver kept glancing at me in his rear-view mirror. He dropped the elderly people off at separate hotels near the waterfront, then snaked through dark city streets that seemed incredibly desolate.

'Do you know where St Georges Terrace is?' I asked.

'We're on it,' he said, laughing.

There was something about his manner that I couldn't stand. It made me want to start listing aloud jobs that were more important than driving a minibus.

The YMCA was just past the hospital. It was a tall grey building with a concrete tennis court out the front. A handful of dishevelled-looking people were congregated near the entrance, smoking. One of them was clutching a portable intravenous stand.

'Do you want me to wait here?' asked the driver after he'd pulled into the car park.

'We'll be fine,' I said, hoping I wouldn't regret it.

There was a young man called Prasad working at the reception desk. He agreed to allocate us a single dormitory. 'The lock's a bit wonky,' he said, handing me the key. 'You've just got to apply a bit of pressure on the cylinder with your thumb.'

We caught the elevator up to the eleventh floor. Harrison kept saying the word 'Prasad' out loud until I told him to stop. I had to swipe a security card to gain entry to the dormitories. Our room was smaller than I had expected. I turned the fan on immediately because Harrison was very sensitive to heat. The carpet was wretched. There was a Holy Bible, a foam cup and three sachets of instant coffee on a fixed bench. I grabbed the cup and walked to the communal kitchen at the end of the hallway, where the shelves were bare except for a microwave and a kettle.

When I returned to the room Harrison was standing by the window, staring through the lattice and counting out loud. I stood beside him and admired the mosaic of lights along the freeway. I thought he might be counting the trucks in the fire station across the street. But there weren't enough. It was only when I noticed his line of vision that I realised he was counting the aeroplanes in the night sky.

Only one channel worked on the television and the screen was fuzzy. I lay on the bed and watched it anyway. *Letterman* was on. When I was young I used to think that David Letterman's drawl was sophisticated beyond belief. Now that I was old I thought he was the least interesting person on the planet. During the ad break after his opening monologue, I noticed that Harrison was riffling through the rubbish bin.

'Jesus Christ, honey!' I yelled. 'It's filthy in there. You know that.'

He stopped without acknowledging that he had heard me. He made his way over to the bed and hopped onto my lap. I rested my head against the wall, which was painted red. It only added to the stuffiness of the room. I switched off the television and sat in the dark, hugging him. I was too tired to force him to brush his teeth. His breathing gradually slowed, which helped me relax. I couldn't remember exactly when I'd let Harrison start sleeping next to me again. It must have been shortly after Eddy left, when I had been faced with the prospect of sleeping alone for the first time in a decade.

■

We sat on the edge of the jetty, away from the seafood outlets and the families dining alfresco, sharing a large paper cup of chips. Harrison hated the smell of the Fremantle fish market. He was a vegetarian because he loved animals. He was always peaceful when he was around them. I had seriously considered adopting a greyhound when I first started working at the veterinary clinic. But I was worried that he might talk to it instead of talking to other children.

'*Miss Rylee!*' he said, reading the name of a navy-blue dinghy that was swaying in the harbour.

The harbour was bustling with restaurants, bars, food stalls and souvenir shops. I could see the top half of a Ferris wheel slowly revolving above the pine trees in the distance. A large group of children in yellow uniforms and floppy hats were sharing fish and chips behind us. It was difficult listening to them discuss the best way to ration their tomato sauce, knowing it was the kind of chat that Harrison would never get to be involved in.

Once we were full we started throwing chips to the seagulls. Harrison didn't have much of an arm on him. When he was in crèche Eddy had observed that sport was never going to be his calling. A crowd of seagulls gathered around us on the jetty. Harrison tried to mimic their squawking.

'You sound happy, Harry.'

'Fight for the potatoes!' he said, flinging dismembered chips onto the planks of the jetty. He was obsessed with potatoes. Aside from sultanas, they were the only food he ate.

When the paper cup was empty we took a walk along the esplanade. We passed market sheds, cargo ships, cruise liners, a ticket booth for the Rottnest ferry and a statue of a man, his daughter and two suitcases. We stopped to admire a vessel that was docked outside the Maritime Museum.

Harrison ran his eyes from the upper deck to the main mast. 'Do you think that's a pirate ship?' he asked.

'It definitely could be.'

'Then where's the Jolly Roger flag?'

'Maybe when pirates come to shore they don't want people to *know* they're pirates anymore.'

Harrison continued to inspect the mast. 'Yes, probably.' His lip curled and he turned the fingers on his right hand into a hook.

I took a detour on our way back to the train station so that I could enjoy some of the restored heritage architecture. Looking at the grand old port buildings and the facades of the bustling hotels, I promised myself that I'd study architecture if I were ever given a second chance at life.

Harrison seemed happy meandering along the footpath in front of me. He eventually stopped outside a large limestone building with a sign above the entrance. The sign had a cartoon of a rooster and bold lettering that read: FREMANTLE HERALD.

'Roosters don't have running shoes.'

'No, of course they don't. I think it's more about what the running shoes symbolise.'

'What do they symbolise?'

'I don't know, honey; let's not get too caught up in this.'

Harrison continued to stare at the rooster with running shoes. It looked remarkably similar to some of his sketches. He was a fantastic sketcher. He always managed to take his subject's most notable features and warp them for comic effect. I had already taken him to a few cartoon studios to show him how people made a career from it. Sketching usually calmed him down. He had a great capacity to absorb information while he was scribbling away on his notepad, even if his teachers thought it was unfair on the other students to permit it in class.

■

I lay on the lawn outside St Mary's Cathedral, soaking up the evening sun. In the last half-hour a refreshing breeze had wafted in from the Swan River, rustling the leaves on the surrounding palm trees. It was a lovely city. Even though it was late autumn, I still didn't need a jumper. I wondered whether it was too hot for Harrison. He always struggled with the long, dry summers back home. As a treat, I sometimes let him run around in the fountains at Victoria Square after school. He was clutching *Peter Pan* and looking at me expectantly.

'I'm ready,' I said.

I closed my eyes and he started to read out loud. He was a beautiful reader. For all the things he didn't understand in this world, he innately understood elocution. He imitated the tick-tock of the crocodile that ate Captain Hook's hand. Our fridge was plastered with sketches of poor old Hook plummeting into the open jaws of a crocodile.

My mind returned, reluctantly, to three days earlier, when I had been summoned to the principal's office. It was the fifth time since the beginning of the term that I'd been forced to leave the clinic mid-shift. I had always wanted Harrison to attend a mainstream school. His intelligence wasn't the issue. He scored fifty-nine out of sixty on the Raven test; most adults couldn't even manage that. Eddy had been vehemently opposed to the idea from the beginning, and every time there was an incident, I could hear his high and mighty lawyer's voice in my head telling me I wasn't living in the real world.

I'd found Harrison sitting in the conference room, immersed in an ancient Vietnamese block game with sentries and prisoners. They always gave him that game to play.

The principal, Ms Donoghue, told me that he had ripped a girl's hijab off in the music room.

'He was obviously overstimulated,' I said. 'We both know he finds music very confronting. There are sounds coming from everywhere and the room's terribly ventilated. Plus that teacher you've got in there is a pushover. All the parents talk about it. I don't even know why you employed him in the first place.'

'No one's mentioned anything to me,' said Ms Donoghue, lying through her teeth.

'I'm telling you, it's chaos in there. Maybe you should pay him a surprise visit sometime and see for yourself. Isn't that what principals are supposed to do?' I realised I wasn't doing myself any favours, but I was so sick of her pretending like she cared and then never following through on anything that we'd talked about.

She called Harrison into her office and asked him why he'd ripped the girl's hijab off.

'Because I wanted to see what Aisha's hair looked like,' he said, understanding from the looks on our faces that remorse was required of him, but not understanding why.

'The first thing I think we should do is write a letter of apology to Aisha's family,' said Ms Donoghue, turning on her friendly voice. 'We don't want these things being blown out of proportion.'

Harrison wrote the letter and gave it to Ms Donoghue.

'Thank you, Harry,' she said, putting it in the top drawer of her desk and turning to address me. 'Now, as I'm sure you're aware, this suspension is going to bring Harrison up to fifteen days in total for the year, which means expulsion is mandatory. Unfortunately our hands are tied on this one.'

She looked at Harrison and spoke to him as if he was a three-year-old. 'Do you understand what that means, Harry?'

He nodded.

When I went to his locker to collect his books, I found it wide open. He'd hoarded eight student diaries.

On the drive home he asked, 'Why is there water coming out of my eyes?'

'. . . *and thus it will go on,*' Harrison read now, '*so long as children are gay and innocent and heartless.*' He closed the book.

I opened my eyes and patted his hair, which was cut shorter than I liked. 'That was fantastic, Harry.'

'The Lost Boys are a bit sad, aren't they?'

'Maybe, but at least they've all found a home.'

He traced his fingers along the cover. 'And lots of friends.'

The lawn had been swallowed by shadows and the breeze had picked up. People were beginning to arrive for evening mass. A young nurse was leaning against the side of the cathedral, fixated on her phone. Her fingers looked manic. The only thing worse than shift work, I wanted to tell her, is a shift that never ends.

■

At 4.06 am Harrison awoke and asked if I could go with him to the toilet. I hadn't managed to get to sleep. The male bathroom was filthy. I felt like I was contracting tinea just by setting foot on the tiles. I settled Harrison in the end cubicle and waited by the open window. Insects milled around the light fittings. I looked out over the cluster of city buildings and listened to the faint ebb of traffic. The lines had almost faded away from the concrete tennis court.

I splashed cold water on my face and studied my complexion in the bathroom mirror. The pouches and wrinkles along my cheeks made me want to cry. It had been years since I bothered to wear make-up. There was no way John the business development manager would even look twice at me now. I wished that I could go back in time to Vanuatu. Everyone in the streets had said hello to us and smiled. I remembered the day Melissa and I took a ferry to Hideaway Island to go snorkelling. She was afraid there were going to be sharks. I couldn't recall being afraid of anything in those days.

What had happened to that fearlessness in me? I wanted to believe that I could get it back and start an eight-hour shift without being frightened to death that my phone was going to start vibrating in my pocket. There were so many other things, too. I wanted to have time to read bestsellers and join a book club and maybe even buy the box set of *Grand Designs*, so I could lie on the couch and laugh at how ludicrous some of the houses were.

Would I ever get to experience the hot smell of whisky on a stranger's breath again? Not that I'd know what to do if I did. Since Eddy had left and Harrison started sleeping in my bed, I hadn't been on a date that had lasted beyond dinner. I didn't even fantasise about it anymore. The only way to recapture that fearlessness was to accept Melissa's offer of a bed in a North Shore apartment and to abandon all sense of care and duty, like I was back in Vanuatu, trying not to think about John's wife and family.

∎

The wide avenues of St Georges Terrace were swarming with traffic. Harrison was keeping a running tally of the taxis that drove by. He was already in the two hundreds. Most of the buildings in the central business district resembled giant shards of glass or giant cheese graters. The only visible exception was a beautiful old colonial building across the street next to a veil of scaffolding. I wished I could run to a local library and read up on its history.

'Hey, Eddy!' I yelled when he appeared at the glass doors of his office building.

It took him a second or two to recognise us, but once he did he walked straight over. I had no idea how I was supposed to greet him. He still looked incredibly handsome in a suit. He crouched down and gave Harrison a big hug.

'Hey, little buddy,' he said, sounding as upbeat as ever. 'Remember me?'

It felt strange watching Harrison hug him back.

Eddy stood up and smoothed his jacket. As he squinted at me, I was relieved to notice the wrinkles at the corners of his eyes.

'What are you two doing here?'

'We came to see you.'

'Right now?'

'Uh-huh,' I said. 'Harry got expelled.'

Harrison started fidgeting with the spine of *Peter Pan*. It was the third copy I'd bought him.

'Are you allowed to take a lunch break or something?' I asked.

He squinted at me again and I wished that I were allowed to get the upbeat facade that he reserved for Harrison. 'Just let me make a call,' he said.

Eddy walked towards a bus shelter and turned his back to us while he spoke on his phone. I felt more offended at that sight than I had when he told me he was applying for a job in another state. He returned with a cheeky grin for Harrison.

'So are we allowed to have a chat?' I asked sarcastically.

'Sure.'

Eddy set off through the city streets. I held Harrison's hand and tried to keep up. We turned right and then left. The sun glared off the glass buildings. Eddy stopped outside a two-storey Victorian pub on the corner of a busy intersection. It was called the Belgian Beer Café. Harrison and I chose a high table in the dining hall while Eddy waited at the main bar. All around us corporate patrons were drinking imported beers and eating mussels.

'Why do they keep ringing the bell?' asked Harrison.

'I think the bartenders ring it every time they get a tip.'

'What sort of tip?'

'It means extra money that's not part of the bill. Money they get to keep for themselves.'

'But not a tip on how to live.'

'No,' I said, smiling. 'Not one of those tips.'

Eddy returned with two glasses of Leffe Blonde and a paper cone filled with chips. He handed the cone to Harrison. 'Be careful, it's hot!' he said.

Harrison started blowing on the chips, eager to impress his dad.

'Where are you staying?' asked Eddy.

'The YMCA.'

'Shit!' said Eddy, leaning across the table and speaking in a hushed voice. 'I've heard it's a dive.'

'I didn't have time to book anywhere.'

He squinted at me, rubbing his lip with his forefinger. I imagined that he regarded his clients in a similar manner.

'I just thought it'd be nice for us both to see you, especially Harry.'

'It is nice,' said Eddy, glancing at Harrison. 'But you should have warned me. That way I could have organised something and freed up a bit more time.'

'What's the matter, are you seeing someone?' The Leffe had gone straight to my head. I hadn't drunk beer in over a year. 'It's alright,' I said. 'I'm not going to be angry.'

Eddy tilted his head in Harrison's direction and smiled. 'Still lord of the fries.'

Harrison was busy blowing on the chips and monitoring their heat with his fingers.

'You appreciate I can't get out of court,' said Eddy.

'I know. I never asked you to.'

'You're putting me in a difficult position.'

His tone made me ache inside. Eddy used to lie next to me in bed at night and tell me all about the cases he was working on. He would show me the interview transcripts of the people he was representing. Sometimes they were thicker than great novels. We would laugh at the policemen's grammar. It was wonderfully unethical. I couldn't help but think that if it wasn't for Harrison, Eddy might still be showing me transcripts in bed.

'I need one year,' I said.

It took Eddy several seconds to understand what I was saying, or asking. His eyes darted towards Harrison. 'Are you sure this is the right place to have this discussion?'

'There's no right place.'

Eddy sipped from his beer.

'It's the last favour I'll ever ask you,' I said, staring at the blurry ceiling lamps.

'I don't know how it can possibly work,' said Eddy.

'But you'll give it a try?'

'Do I have a choice?'

Harrison finally decided that his chips had cooled down enough to begin eating.

'No,' I said.

FORGET
ABOUT
THE PRICES

He was surprised to hear someone knocking on the front door. It was never locked. No one had even given him a house key.

When he answered the door he saw his mother standing on the tatami mat that he'd bought at the local market. She looked much older than the last time he had seen her. It was the skin around her eyes. He wasn't sure how she had managed to find him. The only postcard he had sent was from a sugarcane town several months ago, at the end of the harvest, when he had already booked his next train ticket.

He led her through the weatherboard house to the back porch, where he had been filing his nails. She sat on a wicker couch opposite him and surveyed his Crazy Clark's uniform on the clothesline. It was late in the afternoon. Shadows were creeping across the vegetable garden towards the bungalow where he slept.

'This humidity is something else,' she said, trying to air out her stiff denim vest, which made her look a bit silly. It was nice to hear her voice, though.

'You're looking thin,' she said, eyeing his wrists. 'Am I allowed to buy you dinner tonight?'

■

They ate at a new Japanese restaurant in the main arcade of town. It was deserted.

'Forget about the prices,' said his mother, seeing him inspect the right-hand column of the menu first.

After taking their orders, the Scottish waiter walked outside and fed a handful of dumplings to a pug that was tied up in the passageway. He knew the waiter from somewhere, but it was all a bit foggy and it might just have been because the man had passed through his checkout at some point.

The food tasted rich and nourishing. It was the nicest meal he had eaten in a long time.

'How's your meal?' asked his mum.

'It's good,' he said.

■

After dinner they took a walk along the main street. There were buskers on every corner. The noticeboards were brimming with ads for yoga clinics, drumming workshops, second-hand surfboards and lifts to capital cities with split petrol costs. Backpackers were handing out flyers for the two main nightclubs in town. His mother was too polite to decline the flyers. He didn't visit the nightclubs often. Only when he felt desperate.

She started updating him on the lives of relatives. He knew she'd been dying to do it all evening. One of his cousins had recently got engaged. Another had purchased their first home.

'But the big news is,' she said, unable to contain her excitement any longer, 'you're now an uncle.'

∎

His mother bought them both ice-creams. They walked towards the beach and settled on a grassy knoll. An old, bronze-skinned man with a white beard was approaching strangers on the grass and giving away Hawaiian leis. The man placed one around his mother's neck and kissed her hand, which made her laugh nervously. She looked a bit ridiculous, licking an ice-cream in a denim vest with a colourful necklace on, but she was trying and he knew he couldn't hold it against her.

They sat in silence and watched a lean woman amble across the sand, remove her dress and wade out into the inky ocean. She lay on her back and floated over the waves. Every fifteen seconds her body was fleetingly illuminated by a shaft of light from the distant cliffs.

'I hope she doesn't drown,' said his mother, not daring to take her eyes off the woman.

'It's her own fault if she does,' he said.

A group of fire twirlers started a performance on the grass behind them and a large audience gathered.

'I really like the choreography,' whispered his mother. Her warm breath repulsed him in a way that he knew was unfair. He didn't think there was any choreography.

■

The chirping of the insects grew louder as they drew nearer to the rainforest. His stomach was starting to feel unsettled. They passed several hitchhikers and barely spoke. He knew that his mother was worrying about the young girls with their thumbs out.

When they reached the motel, she stopped and pointed out the blue car she had rented. It didn't really look like her kind of car. He tried not to think about how much money she had spent tracking him down. It would have been much better spent on the new baby.

'Your father would love to teach you how to drive someday,' she said. 'He's been talking about it a lot lately.'

She exhaled when he didn't respond.

'Do you want to come inside for a soft drink?' she asked. 'I think they've got a few different ones in the fridge.'

'Sorry, I'm doing the morning shift tomorrow.'

She suddenly reached over and hugged him. She hugged him for a long time. He didn't feel as though it was his right to relinquish the embrace.

'Do you think you'll come home soon?' she asked.

It was the fake flowers on her necklace that undid him.

'No,' he said, wiping his eyes above her head. 'I'm happy here.'

'No one's ashamed of you,' she said, finally letting go and looking up into his wet eyes. 'I thought it might be important for you to hear it.'

'It is,' he said, sniffling. 'Thanks.'

'Please remember to eat.'

He nodded and she quickly kissed him goodbye.

■

He followed the winding road back towards town. He had got used to wearing thongs at night and he was no longer worried about stepping on cane toads. That was how he knew the Scottish waiter. They had stumbled back to the bungalow together late one night, kicking dead cane toads on the side of the road and laughing.

He approached a big white house with a pristine lawn and a flagpole out the front. He had read about the man who owned the house—a Korean War vet—in the local newspaper. The man woke at seven every morning to raise the country's flag.

He didn't think the man who raised the country's flag every morning would approve of him.

I REMEMBER A TIME
WHEN ONCE
YOU USED TO LOVE ME

Les Holcombe explained the lyrics of the Beatles' song 'Norwegian Wood' to the bartender at the Farmers Arms while his wife Sylvia pretended to survey the interior of the pub. Les had always been good with strangers. He was better with strangers than he was with friends and loved ones. He had entered the congenial fog that usually descended after his third or fourth lowball of scotch. He sometimes gave the impression that he'd prefer to reside within the fog. But like all fogs, it would eventually disperse, leaving him cold and disorientated.

'It was actually the first pop song to use a sitar,' Les was saying. 'George Harrison studied the sitar with Ravi Shankar.'

In his eagerness to engage the bartender—whose accent sounded Irish to Sylvia—Les seemed to have forgotten their purpose in visiting the country. Although it was possible that he knew exactly what he was doing. Still, at least he'd agreed to spend the weekend with her at his brother Dave's holiday house. Given their recent interactions, it seemed like a step in the right direction. It implied that there was hope. The only problem was that she wasn't sure she wanted there to be hope.

Their meals seemed to be taking an eternity. Sylvia had ordered a herb-crusted lamb rack with rocket and grilled pear. She found it odd that a country pub was serving, or trying to serve, such refined cuisine. Dave had warned her that Daylesford was becoming an increasingly upmarket town, pandering to couples on romantic weekend retreats. It was the main reason he'd bought the house. The prices on the chalkboard menu certainly suggested that he'd made a wise investment.

Patrons were scattered throughout the main bar and the crimson-painted dining room. Everyone else at the bar seemed to know one another. Several men were wearing kilts. How on earth were they going to get home? It was freezing outside. When Les had turned off the Midland Highway an hour ago, the thermometer in the Forester had registered an outside temperature of just four degrees.

Les and the bartender had moved on to Van Morrison. If this was his way of putting her to the test, then it wasn't going to achieve anything, even if she did somehow manage to pass. She resented the fact that she now evaluated his actions as though they were so calculated, as though he constantly had revenge on his mind.

Sylvia noticed a laminated newspaper article on the wall. It was about a local footballer who'd been drafted into the national competition. A big smile was splashed across the boy's blotchy cheeks in the accompanying photograph. It reminded her of Les's expression in a photo they'd asked a stranger to take outside the Louvre when they'd been caught in a sudden snowstorm. Neither of them could speak more than five words of French. They were barely even adults then and all they could do was smile at each other.

When their meals finally arrived, Les gathered his cutlery and attacked his Angus fillet. There had always been a primal quality to his eating. When they had first been introduced, in the cafeteria at Monash University, Sylvia had found it endearing. Her lamb was nice and tender, but the pear was too sweet. She just wanted to say it out loud. Why couldn't Les stop chewing with his mouth open and say something?

'So, what films do you want to see?' she asked finally. She removed the program for the Melbourne International Film Festival from her purse and spread it across the bar.

'I'm not fussed,' said Les.

'Has anything taken your fancy?'

Les glanced at the program. 'I haven't really given it much thought this year.'

'There's a South Korean film I've been dying to see. You'd like it, I think. It's set in Seoul.'

Les attracted the bartender's attention and signalled for another scotch.

'We saw the preview together earlier this year,' said Sylvia, wondering whether it was before or after she'd started sleeping with her boss. 'It was set in the snow and everything was in reverse.'

'Really?' said Les, staring at a small axe that was suspended above the bar. 'I can't remember it.'

One of the purple-cheeked men wearing a kilt erupted into laughter and thrust his pint towards the ceiling, almost spilling beer on Sylvia.

'Do you want to see the film or not?' she asked. 'It's on Friday week at the Forum.'

'Sure, whatever you want.'

'I want what you want.'

'Great.'

■

Sylvia was woken the next morning by rasping music coming from the kitchen. She put on her dressing gown and opened the curtains, admiring the golden fur on the branches of the walnut tree in the backyard. A white net had been draped over the tree to prevent the cockatoos from eating Dave's walnuts. Dave didn't care about walnuts, but he maintained that life wasn't worth living without engaging in such warfare with animals. It was probably why he'd been divorced three times.

The central heating had been turned on. She stood above the vent near the window, letting the warm air caress her legs. She didn't know what to make of the house. The furnishings were more modern than she'd expected and there were ugly Warhol prints all over the bedroom walls. When Dave first suggested the retreat, she'd imagined a cottage in the woods with an open fireplace. She couldn't help but resent the dishwasher, the clothes dryer and even the central heating unit just a little.

Dave had purchased the house from an oncologist who had built it with retirement in mind. The oncologist had found a melanoma on his own neck eighteen months before he was due to retire. He passed away six days after the settlement period had ended. Ever since, Dave had referred to him as 'the dying doctor'. For some reason it always made Sylvia laugh.

Les was making scrambled eggs and listening to Dirty Three. Sylvia knew the album. It was called *Horse Stories*, which she suspected was a reference to some illicit drug. There weren't even any vocals on the album, just drums, electric guitar and violin. She was prepared to concede that there was a profound sadness in the wailing of the violin, but she found it all a bit disconcerting.

The violinist, Warren Ellis, was a deranged expatriate who lived in Paris. Les had shown her pictures of his beard. She didn't trust an urban bushranger with her husband's heart.

Les was busy distributing the scrambled eggs onto toasted sourdough bread. His shirtsleeves were rolled up and there were damp patches underneath his armpits.

'Where'd you get the eggs?' asked Sylvia.

'There's a farmers' market down at the primary school. They've got everything.' He gestured with the silicon flipper towards two glasses of freshly squeezed orange juice. 'I also got fudge.' He smiled eagerly, like a six-year-old boy.

'I might wander down there after breakfast to have a look,' she said. 'What should we do for dinner?' She was keen to eat a home-cooked meal so that Les couldn't become best friends with the waiter and block her out again. At some point they were actually going to have to talk about it.

'I'm easy,' he said.

He placed their plates on the dining table. A raucous violin solo coursed from the stereo. Les had once told her that Warren Ellis liked to attach a guitar pickup to his violin to distort the instrument's traditional sound.

'Is there any chance you can turn that down?' she asked.

'Sure,' said Les. He switched off the stereo and brought over the two glasses of orange juice.

'I got two flavours,' he said, taking the seat opposite her.

'Of what?'

'Fudge. I got two different flavours. Jaffa and peppermint.'

■

They followed a damp path that wound through a plantation of conifers and led to an observation tower in the middle of the Botanic Gardens. Les had to stop halfway up the spiral staircase to catch his breath. It was strange for Sylvia watching him hunched over, clutching the rail. He used to go for an evening run three times a week before he set out on this course of self-destruction. She knew it was her fault and that any normal person would have felt guilty; not that a normal person would have driven Les to it in the first place, but she couldn't help thinking that he was hamming it up.

At the summit there was a wonderful panoramic view of the township and the tree-lined expanse that spilt towards the Great Dividing Range. But they only got to spend a few minutes admiring it before a young German couple arrived and started taking photographs all around them.

They made their way cautiously down the staircase and crossed an old railway bridge on the other side of the gardens. Sylvia was sick of being the one to break the silence, so she didn't. They soon came across a small shopping strip that had a handcrafted furniture gallery, a wine bar, a nursery and an acupuncturist. Even though Sylvia knew it was all nonsense, she no longer felt put off by the idea of a stranger sticking needles all over her back. It was probably the least she deserved.

'Should we go back to school?' asked Les, smiling like a boy again and pointing at a sign to a secondary school.

The school was a little further up the road, opposite a chain of modern townhouses. They inspected the grounds and stopped at the football oval, which was on a slope. Sylvia settled on the bottom tier of the portable aluminium seating beside the oval.

'Dave said something funny recently,' said Les, surveying the pastures in the distance that were tinged with maroon. 'He said when they were getting evacuated a few summers ago, all the neighbours were running around, loading up their cars with photos and valuables. He said he decided he might as well just drive off. The house and everything in it would either burn or not burn.'

Les laughed, but not completely. 'That's exactly how he said it, *burn or not burn*. As he was driving back to the city, the thing he kept thinking was, *what's the worst that can happen?* As long as he got to keep his life, and got to keep on signing divorce papers, he didn't feel too fussed about any of it.'

Les walked over to Sylvia and looked her in the eye. 'In my good moments now, that's what I keep trying to remind myself. What's the worst that can happen?' he said, taking hold of her hand. 'I know there are worse things than this.'

'Of course there are,' she said, feeling relieved that he was finally opening up.

'And if we can just find a way through this, it might start to get a bit easier at some point.'

'Is that what you want?'

'Right now it is,' said Les, letting go of her hand. 'But if you'd asked me last night or any time in the last few weeks, you probably would've got a different answer.'

He crouched down and ran his fingers through the brown grass. 'I don't know what stops I'd wear if I was playing on here,' he said. 'Probably screw-ins, just to be on the safe side.'

'You wouldn't get a game in your condition.'

Les's cheeks started going red, but he smiled. It was heartening to see him smile properly.

'Why don't you come back over here?' she said.

Les stood up and sat next to Sylvia. After a minute or two he leant in and kissed her. She didn't feel like resisting any longer. She wrapped her hands around his thick, greying hair and pulled him on top of her. He frantically unfastened his belt buckle and started breathing deeply. It was nice to have finally roused some life within him. His cheeks were prickly and his breath was warm and yeasty. She wanted to tell him to soften his groans, but no one else could hear them. Les worked away, just like he had the previous evening on his Angus fillet. He knew what he wanted. It was frightening how much he still wanted it.

■

'We have several private treatments available today,' said the receptionist at the Hepburn Spa.

She was a young woman, barely twenty. Sylvia wondered whether Les liked her frizzy blond hair, which was tied back in a ponytail. Not that Sylvia had any right to be jealous.

'We'll just take two normal tickets,' said Les, looking at the receptionist a little longer than Sylvia thought was necessary.

'Alright, sir. That will give you access to the communal relaxation pool and the spa.'

'Sounds perfect.' Les removed his wallet from his trouser pocket.

'For an extra forty dollars you can have access to the Sanctuary.'

'The Sanctuary,' said Les, grinning pathetically. 'Sounds like a bloody housing estate.'

The receptionist laughed. She seemed to mean it. 'It's an adults-only section of the facility with an aroma steam room and a salt therapy pool.'

'I think we'll live without it,' said Les, before leaning over the desk and whispering, 'but thanks for trying.'

He sounded ridiculous. Sylvia thought they were beyond playing games. If there really were so many possibilities for him, why was he wasting his time listening to Dirty Three and writing himself off every night? Why didn't he just make a clean break and groan into the ears of stuck-up twenty-year-olds until his heart was content?

After changing into her bathers, Sylvia decided that she wouldn't wait for Les and went straight into the relaxation pool. The water was warmer than she'd expected. She waded towards a feature wall at the far end of the pool and settled against a blue-tiled pillar. Daylight streamed through the large rectangular windows. She stared at her distorted feet on the bottom of the pool. She'd been looking forward to visiting Hepburn Springs for years. Now that she'd arrived—now that her flesh was finally being 'soothed' by magnesium—it all felt a bit underwhelming.

Lead a double life. That's how the Tourism Victoria ads on TV had tried to sell Daylesford. Could they have possibly come up with a more moronic angle? What Sylvia really wanted was to see the young woman depicted on the ads in five or six months' time, when she was immersed in all of the things that she'd tried to run away from in the first place.

Sylvia felt like urinating in the pool. No one would notice. But it was the kind of senseless urge that had got her into trouble in the first place. She still had no idea why she'd acted on it. Sometimes a course of action presented itself and it felt like it made no difference whether she went along with it or whether she put a stop to it. The stupid thing was that if Les knew how insignificant the whole fling with her boss had been, from start to finish, he probably wouldn't even care about it.

Les entered the poolside area with a hired towel wrapped around his waist and headed straight for the spa. The hairs on his chest were pasted across his pectoral muscles, which were beginning to lose definition. Sylvia felt like she was watching a stranger. Funny, since those were almost the exact words that Les had levelled at her the night she finally built up the courage to tell him. 'I feel like I'm talking to a total stranger,' he'd said. Then he'd stormed out of the house and come back three days later with scotch on his breath.

Sylvia joined Les in the spa. His eyes were half-closed and his mouth was wide open. She sat against an underwater jet that pulsed against her lower vertebrae, observing an elderly couple sitting on the opposite side of the spa. The skin on their faces looked pale, dry and stretched. No matter how hard she tried, it was impossible to picture herself at their age. She closed her eyes and listened to the popping of the bubbles. When she was on the cusp of dozing off, she felt Les's hand cup her right breast. He manipulated it rigorously, as though he was a baker kneading a handful of dough, and gave her nipple a pinch. She opened her eyes. He still wasn't even looking at her.

She brushed his hand away and he didn't try it again.

■

Sylvia sat on the back porch, sipping tea and staring at the creamy-pink magnolias that surrounded the wooden decking.

She could smell lavender from one of the neighbours' gardens. It was a cold, overcast morning. Dew blanketed the grass in the backyard. Les was still asleep. They had planned on spending the morning in Ballarat, where one of the local galleries had an exhibition of political cartoons, but she was starting to doubt that it was going to happen. The original Eureka Flag was also on display at the gallery. Les had always loved reading about Lalor, Carboni and the Eureka Stockade.

He'd stopped reading as well as running, which struck her as a huge shame. It was all about gloomy music now. On previous holidays they'd invented a system of sharing the same book, whereby Les—who was the faster reader—would start the book first, finish the opening chapter, rip out the clump of pages and give them to Sylvia. As he read on, he'd continue to rip out the chapters one at a time. To friends they often joked that a good book wasn't just a page-turner, it was also a page-ripper.

Sylvia didn't want to think about the past anymore, so she turned on the central heating and had a long shower in the downstairs bathroom. The whole house was nice and toasty by the time she'd finished. She stood by the vent in the kitchen, wrapped in a red towel that she'd found in one of the built-in robes. Les had forgotten to pack their towels, even though it was the only thing she'd specifically asked him to remember. A glass was upturned on the floorboards. She picked it up and noticed that the rim was chipped. It was only now that she recollected being briefly awakened by loud rummaging in the kitchen during the night.

Les emerged at the bottom of the stairs. He rubbed his stubble and groaned.

'Would you like some lunch?' she asked.

Les shook his head and shivered. 'Listen, my head's throbbing,' he said croakily. 'I'm not going to make it to the exhibition.' He glanced at the red towel and gave Sylvia a look that she found a little histrionic.

'Why don't we go to the lake instead?' she said. 'We could take a walk and browse at the book barn and drink some coffee.'

'No, sorry, I just came down to see if there was any Panadol.'

'Come on, the fresh air might do you good.'

He glanced at the red towel again. 'You can go by yourself if you want.'

'I don't want to go by myself.'

His body was exuding a strong scent that was becoming far too familiar for her liking.

'The idea is to do things together,' said Sylvia.

'You'll have to forgive me. I don't seem to know the protocol as well as you.'

'There's no protocol.'

That was precisely the problem. She felt like an idiot for allowing herself to believe that a weekend in the country could make even the slightest difference.

'Sorry,' said Les.

'I don't want you to be sorry.'

'Someone has to be.'

He studied her exposed collarbones. 'That suits you.'

'What?' she asked.

'The red towel, it suits your skin colour.'

'Thanks.'

They stared at each other. Sylvia visualised Dave saying 'the dying doctor' with malevolent glee all over his cheeks. She had to bite down on her cheeks to refrain from laughing.

■

Once Les had retreated to the upstairs bedroom, Sylvia decided to go for a drive. It didn't matter where. When she turned the key in the ignition, the car stereo burst to life. The volume was almost deafening. She instantly recognised the faux-waltz opening of the fourth track from *Horse Stories*. The clamorous rhythm of the snare steadily increased as she joined a courteous stream of traffic on the outskirts of town. She didn't know half as much as Les about drums, but she felt certain that the snare was deliberately out of tune. She turned left without indicating at a roundabout on the main street and pressed her bare foot on the accelerator.

She soon found herself hurtling along a bumpy road in the foothills of town. Each snare roll, each surge in feedback, each jarring excretion from the violin, compelled her to press her foot harder on the accelerator. It was more fun than staring at cartoons. She tried to induce her limbs to act of their own volition, determining the speed at which the Forester took each corner without allowing her mind to interfere with the outcome.

The vehicle veered onto the wrong side of the road as it approached a sharp corner. Sylvia clutched the steering wheel and plunged her foot down, desperate to find the brake. The tyres screeched. Or was it the violin? It now sounded like a horse was being tortured to death. The vehicle swivelled. The road and the landscape blurred. Everything felt weightless. But before the end could come, the tyres regained traction. She pulled onto the tall grass at the side of the road and shakily cut the engine.

She got out of the car and was surprised by how unsteady she felt on her feet when she tried to walk. The stench of burning rubber was sickening. She had to stop and lean against a sheltered partition to regain her breath. Once she'd finished gasping, she realised that the partition was actually an unattended roadside stall. Several tubs of honey were lined up on a wooden bench. She felt compelled to take one, even though she didn't have her purse handy. There didn't seem to be a camera anywhere. What did it matter even if someone did see her? *Lead a double life*, wasn't that the slogan?

■

A pamphlet had been left under the front door, advertising a three-day convention in Bendigo the following month. The convention was going to include a full costume Bible drama and an audio demonstration of a Bible account, whatever that meant. Sylvia toyed with the notion of setting the pamphlet alight, but instead opted to put it in the recycling bin.

Les was sitting at the dining table in front of four empty clip-top bottles, eating fudge. He was clean-shaven. 'What's that?' he asked calmly, eyeing the tub of honey in her hand.

'I got it for Dave, to say thank you.'

'Great idea,' he said, biting into the fudge and chewing with his mouth open. 'He always liked you.'

Sylvia didn't know what to say in response. The words sounded so finite.

'Are you still keen for a walk?' asked Les.

'Of course.'

They both put on padded Gore-Tex jackets and grabbed two empty bottles. The air had a country chill to it. They descended a steep hill and followed a gravel road that was lined with brush. Les found an opening along the fence line of a nearby property. A muddy path led towards two rotting pallets and a mineral spring in front of a dilapidated miner's cottage.

Les positioned one of the glass bottles underneath the spring, which had been repaired with electrical tape and cable ties. When the bottle was full, he handed it to Sylvia. He filled the remaining bottles and they started walking back up the hill towards the house. He was moving faster than usual and it was a strain to keep up.

'What did it feel like?' asked Les suddenly, keeping his eyes glued to the road. 'I mean, during it, what did it actually feel like?'

'Do you really want me to answer that?'

'It's fine, it doesn't matter now.' He exhaled sharply, producing a small white cloud. 'I've obviously thought about it too, you know. There was a woman at the office a few years ago, she was only a temp, but there were times I thought the whole balance of my day was in her eyes.'

He looked intently at Sylvia before wiping his brow and returning his gaze to the road. 'Anyway, nothing ever happened. But I thought about it. I couldn't stop thinking about it. The problem was, I couldn't imagine actually going through with it without breaking down into tears. That's what I don't understand. How did you manage to do it without crying?'

'I don't know,' said Sylvia. She'd never thought of it like that, but she would've preferred it if she'd been able to cry at some point.

'It felt like nothing,' she found herself saying. 'I don't know if that's what you want to hear or not, but it's true. It all just felt like nothing.'

'But there must have been something about him that you were attracted to.'

'No, really, there wasn't.'

'Then why do it?'

'I honestly don't know,' she said, suddenly feeling the full weight of the glass bottles. 'It was just a stupid, senseless thing to do. Once we started, or once I started, there was no point stopping. If there was ever something I wanted out of it, rest assured, I certainly didn't get it.'

They walked a little further up the hill, past a rectangular pink house that looked like a life-size doll's house. Next to the pink house was an enormous timber structure with a portable toilet out the front.

'Do you remember that time outside the Louvre?' she asked, trying to suck as much oxygen into her lungs as she could. 'When we got stuck in the snow.'

'Of course, I was freezing my balls off.'

'We were in love then, weren't we?'

'Yes we were, or I was anyway.'

'I was too,' she said. 'You know that.'

They kept on walking. A low mist enveloped the cypresses near the summit of the Botanic Gardens. Sylvia's arms felt so heavy that she thought they might drop off.

'I'm not coming to the South Korean film,' said Les.

THE GREATEST
SHOWBAG
ON EARTH

Josh starts nagging us to walk faster the second we get through the turnstiles. He doesn't know what it means to work on your feet five days a week, just to blow half a day of wages on admission. He wants to go straight to the showbag pavilion, probably because he's never had to deal with the throng of sweaty outer-suburban bodies himself. Like most unpleasant things in this world, that's my job.

'If we buy the showbags now,' I explain, putting on the stern paternal voice that I hardly believe in anymore myself, 'we'll have to carry them around with us all day and the chocolate will melt in the sun.'

'No it won't,' he fires back. 'I'll just eat it now.'

'It'll make you sick.'

'Bullshit.'

This is the first time he's sworn at me. There's been eight months straight of dissent and I see now that it's all been building to this blunt retort. I know that just by weighing up how to respond, I'm already losing his respect. If there's any left. I have half a mind to clip him over the ear, but I don't want to do it in front of Charlotte or any of the other ghastly families in the vicinity, because then they'll mistake me for the bad guy.

'I'm the one who makes the money in this family,' I say, panting, 'so I'll decide when we get to spend it, bullshit or not.'

That shuts him up.

The showbag pavilion is already packed to the rafters. If there is a hell, I'd bet good money that it's an eternal showbag pavilion. I'm tempted to bore straight in there and buy Josh his showbags now, so he can try to eat all his chocolate at once and end up vomiting. Then I'll say, 'I told you so.' Or not even say it. Just let him struggle around in the sun all day, chocolate drunk, and not say a thing.

Fi always used to wait with the kids while I waded through the human crush to buy overpriced chocolate bars and Asian-made toys that'd be lucky to last a month. I realise that I'll either have to leave the kids standing outside the pavilion unsupervised, or get them to brave it with me. Neither is a good option. I can't wait until those showbags are in my hands at the end of the day. Then we can find the car, which is parked in the front yard of a

73

Chinese family who are making a killing off this bloody thing, and it'll all be over for another year.

I can't even remember what their showbag allowance is supposed to be. Are they allowed three showbags each or have they got forty dollars each to spend? Charlotte always likes to get the Bertie Beetle showbag. I remember that much. But it's probably the cheapest thing in all of Homebush and it'd be unfair if it counted as a whole showbag. That was another thing Fi always took care of. I never realised how we'd divided all the things in our life into such clear jurisdictions. It feels like every week I'm discovering systems that used to be in place.

There are prams and balloons and marching bands and face-painting stalls and food outlets all around us. I know the idea is to embrace the festivity, and maybe I did once, but all I can think about now is the petrol, the parking, the price of admission, the rides, the hot chips and God knows what other expenses that might pop up. Are they charging us to use the toilets yet?

Mum gave me one hundred dollars last night to put towards the show. It really pissed me off. I know I'll spend the money, because my pride isn't worth taking fairy floss out of the kids' mouths. There was genuine pity in the way she closed my hand around the two yellow notes, not even expecting a thank you, like this was how life was going to be from now on. I never planned on being an object of pity. Who does? But once you are—once

people start looking at you with that pained, sympathetic smile—
it feels like a long, long road back.

■

I proposed to Fi on a Saturday evening in Centennial Park, just
before the fruit bats started going berserk. A colleague at the
brewery had suggested the location. We packed a picnic and
sat in the shade by the water. Young children were flying kites
and climbing the fig trees around us. I couldn't think of a more
perfect park in the whole world.

It was funny in a way, sitting there all afternoon, knowing
what I wanted to ask, but still feeling nervous about it, trying to
find the perfect moment. Nowadays I think there is no perfect
moment. I remember the way the wind was blowing Fi's hair
across her eyes and her talking about how she'd love to live in
one of the houses with big wrought-iron gates overlooking the
park. She said the whole park could be our kids' playground.
I felt so proud knowing that such a beautiful woman wanted
to be the mother of my children. If I'd had any sense, I would
have come out with it right then and there.

Fi suggested that we take a walk to get away from all the kids
and the weekend revellers. As we were walking beneath the
paperbark trees, I realised that I was behaving like a teenager on
his first date, trying to keep the conversation flowing, wondering
if he's going to pinch a goodnight kiss. I won't pretend I didn't

need to shit. It was absurd, because I knew Fi—or thought I did—and we'd already shared the most intimate moments of my life.

We ended up at one of the cricket ovals, watching the end of a match. All those men dressed in white, shouting out nonsense to each other, it seemed like a pointless exercise to me. Eventually, as the players were collecting the cones, I reached into my pocket and put my hand on the ring box. My words didn't sound as momentous as I'd hoped. Fi started laughing, which was the one response I wasn't expecting. She told me she'd found the ring in my bedside drawer a few weeks ago when she was looking for batteries. But the answer was still yes.

■

The sun is already oppressive. I realise that I've forgotten to pack the sunscreen. Not that the kids care. They're already surveying the carousels, the revolving teacups, the rollercoasters, and the people dangling from giant robotic arms, screaming as one. I'm stunned by how much the rides cost. Isn't the Minister for Fair Trading supposed to keep an eye on these things? I'd like to boycott all of them. But that'll just give Josh even more ammunition the next time he starts whingeing about what a cheapskate I am.

'Can we please go on the Haunted Hotel?' asks Charlotte, squeezing my hand.

'It's not even scary,' says Josh.

I see Charlotte instantly change her mind.

I know I shouldn't think of an eleven-year-old as my enemy, particularly one I helped to raise, but Josh's insistence on making every day an ordeal for the three of us is as big a crime as any that's been committed. I don't know what he thinks he's achieving by doing it and I'd be surprised if he knew. It's hard to believe he hugged me when I gave him a Rabbitohs footy on his eleventh birthday.

A group of boys in their early teens are mocking the man driving the miniature railway. 'Don't trust him in that tunnel,' says one of them. His friends give him a round of high-fives, as though it's the wittiest thing that's ever been said. The driver is managing to stay in character, but I can tell it's getting to some of the parents. What's the world coming to? If there's any justice, the boys will learn firsthand what a child molester is sometime soon. That'd shut them up.

The worst thing is, I know it's a phase that Josh is going to pass through too. I can already see it in him. That dumb mob mentality. Then there'll be Charlotte's teen years. I don't even want to think about those. The energy it's going to take, just trying to hold everything together for the two of them. I don't think it's in me. I can't even figure out how I'm going to summon the energy to make it through today.

'How about a quick walk through the nursery?' I say,

remembering how Charlotte used to love feeding cups of hay to the baby goats.

'It stinks in there,' says Josh.

I look to Charlotte for support, but I can tell she doesn't want to stand up to Josh.

'This is why the show actually started,' I say, pointing angrily at the nursery, 'to let the country people show off their lifestyle to city people like us.'

They're not interested. I can hear Fi's voice in my head, telling me for the umpteenth time not to lecture them.

I let Charlotte play the laughing clowns instead, even though she's got no idea how to factor in the delay between dropping the ping pong balls and when they funnel into the numbered rows. It's infuriating to watch. I try not to start calculating how much of my weekly wage each ball is worth. Josh convinces Charlotte to let him drop the last few balls in the clown's mouth, but even he can't seem to figure out the timing.

The carny—a thin man with gaunt features and sport sunglasses—flicks me a sympathetic smile. I know he's faking it because I'm used to the real thing. I don't know how he sleeps at night, charging what he does, but I'm sure it's with a heap of heroin in his veins. Even though he doesn't realise it, we're united in this moment. I too am relieved that Charlotte hasn't scored enough points to win a major prize, because it means I don't have to carry a big stuffed unicorn around all day.

∎

I watch Josh and Charlotte climb the rainbow slide, carrying their magic carpets. I sit on a bench, enjoying every second off my feet. Parenting is an ongoing equation of time spent on feet subtracted by time spent off feet to determine a state of mind. Josh thinks I fake the pain. Right now he's not moving any quicker than I do, trudging up the stairs, making a point of showing me how lame he thinks the slide is. Why can't he just work with me today? We're all in it together. We all wish it could be just like last year.

The thing I remember best from last year is the four of us watching the woodchopping. I know it meant nothing to the kids, but it was always Fi's favourite part of the show. A young Tasmanian kid—he can't have been older than sixteen—was going up against his dad in a heat of the tree-felling. The old man gave him a good thirty-second head start. One of the other axemen was already started on the second side of his pole. I said, 'He'll never catch them,' and Fi said, 'Let's just wait and see.' She was right. The old man pipped his son and the other bloke right at the finish.

All I want today, the one thing I want to do for myself, if that's such a crime, is to watch ten minutes of the woodchopping. It's funny how someone like Fi, who couldn't give two shits about sport, was always so fascinated by the tree-felling. I never

79

bothered to ask her why, but my guess is it was the thrill of watching the axemen climb their poles and hack away at their blocks, balancing on those wobbly planks, knowing they could fall at any minute.

The kids are at the top of the slide now. I study the scattering of clouds above the football stadium and hope they're going to bring rain. The kids set off at the same time, but Charlotte picks up more speed than Josh. Her high-pitched screaming is the only sound I hear in the whole showgrounds. I watch her small, innocent body ride the pink undulations and I realise why I love her the most. She's the only person I know who looks at me and doesn't see an object of pity.

∎

I've thought about killing myself. I know it's not a healthy sign. I've even started thinking about how I'd do it. There's a big difference between planning it and actually going through with it, even if the online doctors say you should seek help immediately if you've started considering the logistics of it.

There's a train station on the Illawarra line. It's the stop before we get off to visit my parents every Friday night. There are only two platforms. As far as I can tell, it's pretty quiet. I'd never do it at peak hour, disrupting all those innocent commuters, making thousands of people late for work. We've got enough congestion problems as it is in this city. I'd do it late at night, after I've put the kids to bed and packed their lunchboxes, when no one's life would really be inconvenienced.

■

I try to build up the nerve to talk to Josh as we're queuing up for the dodgem cars. He's still pissed off about the showbags and having to go on the rainbow slide with Charlotte. He'd rather go on Free Fall, No Limit, Power Surge, the Zipper and every other ride that's probably going to end with an investigation from the coroner's office. But it's not going to happen on my watch.

'You happy to drive by yourself, big man?' I say, pretending everything's rosy between us.

'Obviously,' he says, not even looking at me.

I can't stand the self-consciousness. Doesn't he realise that no one's watching him, assessing his reaction to everything I say in case he gives even the slightest hint that he loves me? Would it be such a crime to love me?

There are about thirty people in front of us in the queue. I try to calculate our chances of getting through in the next group. It'll be tight. Charlotte is tugging on my sleeve and trying to inch forwards. I'm not sure what else she expects when she insists on coming here. At least we're not asylum seekers. I look at the family in front of us, all decked out in their Holden gear, and I could swear that this is fun to them. They probably can't wait to go to Bathurst later this year and camp out with all those other rev heads. Ford versus Holden, who gives a shit?

We make it through to the racing track and there's hardly any space between the dodgem cars. They've packed it even tighter than last year. But that's the way it's all going. Less space equals more money. I fasten Charlotte's seatbelt. I'm counting on this being another respite for me, driving around to the monotony of Top Forty music, enjoying being off my feet for the stingy few minutes that they afford us.

The music starts and the attendant tells us to drive in an anti-clockwise direction. I swerve around a mother–daughter combination, narrowly avoiding their rear bumper, and I can feel a smile working its way across my rigid lips. I squeeze Charlotte's shoulder. She keeps saying, 'Watch out, Dad!' as though our lives depend on it. We get our first nudge from another car and it sends a pinch of pain down the left side of my neck. The fun is over.

Josh is stuck in the corner, spinning his steering wheel around furiously. An attendant hops onto his bonnet, grabs the wheel and helps him reverse out of trouble. We get banked up in traffic on the opposite side of the track. We're at other people's mercy now, wedged sideways between cars. I see Josh coming straight for us. There's menace in his eyes. I have just enough time to brace Charlotte for the impact, but she still screams right in my ear as he cannons into the side of us.

■

We finally get a respite from the sun in the food dome. This is my one chance to save money. The kids both take sample slices of Granny Smiths from the Woolworths stall and I feel instantly relieved that they're eating fruit. That's one jurisdiction that was never mine: enforcing the consumption of fruit and vegetables. Nowadays Josh will only eat vegetables if he can put tomato sauce on them.

We move on to the dukkah stall, but Charlotte says it all tastes like bird food. The two pieces of bread I manage to cram into my mouth are bursting with flavour, but what do I know? The kids are more excited about eating sour watermelon straps. I already know they're going to hate me when I refuse to buy any for them. The woman at the stall senses it and doesn't give me too much of a sales pitch. Even total strangers are getting into the swing of pitying me.

'Why can't we just buy one thing?' asks Josh, putting on the whiniest voice I've ever heard. 'You're such a tight-arse.'

I don't even bother with a retort.

I notice the cramped stall that our brewery has set up. A bearded kid in a black apron is flogging one of our new craft beers. I'm tempted to grab a sample and hear his spiel. But the beer tastes a bit fruity for my liking. It's more for the hipsters in Surry Hills. Besides, it'd take about two hundred and fifty of those small plastic cups to get me to where I want to be right now.

At the chilli stall, the samples are ranked out of ten in terms of heat. I challenge Josh to a friendly competition. We start at the Kangaroo Punch, which is ranked six out of ten, and scoop it onto our rice crackers. When we get to the Dragon's Blood, I feign that I'm struggling, for Charlotte's sake.

'Keep going, Dad!' she says, looking genuinely concerned for my wellbeing.

We move on to the Taipan Venom. Whoever comes up with the names for the flavours is actually doing a commendable job. Not that it's even about the flavour anymore. Why would anyone in their right mind want to buy any of these? I can tell Josh is feeling the heat. So am I, but I'm not going to let him win. There's one thing he's forgetting: I don't care what happens to me.

'That's not going to be much fun on the way back out,' says the attendant to Josh as he's trying the Scorpion Strike, which is ranked fifteen out of ten. I see a glimmer of panic flash across his face.

I know I've got him beaten.

■

I was at a hops farm in the Derwent Valley when Fi called to tell me she was pregnant. My reception wasn't great, but I heard her say something about baby names. I started running between the bines, past all the bright green cones, trying to find a spot where I could hear her properly. By the time I finally got an extra bar of reception, she sounded so calm and devoid of joy. I assumed it was because she'd had time to absorb the magnitude of the news.

I didn't learn much about sourcing hops to the North American market that afternoon. The whole time they were leading us around the farm and through the picking shed, I was lost in my own thoughts, trying to wrap my head around the news. At the end of the tour, I went for a walk on the farm. They were mid-harvest. I felt like I could keep walking forever, playing with all the possibilities in my head. The one thing I resolved was that I'd give the kid the greatest life anyone had ever known.

■

We sit in the shade of the grandstand. My hips are killing me. The officials are raking the lawn after a heat of the standing block. A few of the tree-felling axemen are inspecting the large poles on the far side of the arena. Josh is eating a cup of hot chips and Charlotte is eating a deep-fried potato on a stick. I haven't eaten since the food dome. That chilli isn't sitting too well. But it doesn't matter. For once, I'm relaxed.

The announcer introduces the six axemen competing in the next heat. One of them is the Tasmanian kid from last year.

He hasn't put on much weight. Looking at him, you wouldn't think he had it in him. There are two New Zealanders, one man from Queensland, one from Victoria and one from New South Wales. I ask Charlotte who her money is on and she picks the Queenslander because he's got the biggest muscles.

'One . . . two . . . three!' says the announcer.

The crowd starts cheering as the Tasmanian kid plants his first board in its pocket. Chips of wood are flying everywhere. You've got to appreciate the strength and the endurance of these men. I'm sure they don't make much of a living from it. The Queenslander finishes the first half of his block. The Tasmanian kid is making up serious ground on him. I find myself clenching my fists and barracking for the kid out loud. I can't remember the last time I got this excited about anything.

'Dad,' says Charlotte, raising her voice to be heard, 'I think I cut my mouth on the stick.'

I glance at her and she scrunches her face up. 'You look fine to me,' I say.

'It hurts.'

'Can you hold on for just a minute?' I ask, as the Tasmanian kid starts leaping nimbly down his boards, collecting them as he goes.

I look back and see her probing her mouth with her thumb. She pulls it out and there's the slightest trace of blood. It's enough to send her over the edge. I should have known it was too good to last.

'It really hurts,' she says, eyes welling with tears.

'Okay, okay, let's go and find the St John van,' I say. 'Keep your fingers out of there.'

'Finally,' says Josh, the little shit.

I apologise to the people in our row as we block their views on our way past. Charlotte is already wailing, thinking she's gaining sympathy. I can hear blocks of wood being hacked into and the crowd getting louder all around us, but I don't even want to look. The one thing I do see, to my disbelief, is Josh drop his paper cup on the stairs and keep walking.

■

The kids' faces are already pink. They're telling me what showbags they want. I'm trying to repeat them in my head so I don't stuff it up and incur any more of Josh's wrath. Peppa Pig, Starburst Super Bag, Bertie Beetle, Cadbury Favourites, Hubba Bubba and the Greatest Showbag on Earth. But if they've sold out of the dart rifle, Josh wants the M&M's Family Bag instead. Instead of what? Has it always been this complicated or is my memory deteriorating?

'Please wait here,' I say.

I look at Josh. You're a big kid now, my look is telling him. This is a watershed moment. Embrace its importance and don't knife me in the back like you've been doing nonstop for the past eight months.

'Okay, Dad,' he says, like there's no reason for me to doubt his commitment to the cause.

'Make sure you stay with your brother,' I tell Charlotte. She's forgotten all about her mouth now. 'I'll be back soon. I want to see you both standing right here when I come back. In this spot.'

I can already hear the collective murmur of the showbag pavilion. It'll be a miracle if I get through it without murdering someone.

'Hey, Dad,' says Charlotte. 'When's Mum getting back from her holiday?'

I feel like someone has stabbed a dozen knives into the gaps of my ribcage and left them all jammed in there.

'I don't know,' I manage to say.

'What do you mean?'

My top lip is trembling and I already know that Josh will never respect me again. But when I look up, expecting to see his scathing expression, there are tears in his eyes. He can't even look at me. The last thing I feel like doing anymore is leaving them.

'Tell you what, Charlie,' I say, getting down on one knee. 'Why don't we forget about the showbags for now? On the way home I'll stop at the supermarket and the two of you can spend a hundred dollars on lollies and chocolate and anything else you want. Then we can all go home and make the greatest showbag on earth together.'

'But I really want a Peppa Pig backpack for school,' she says.

'I'm sure we can track one of those down somewhere at DFO,' I say, pretending I've considered it.

'No, it has to come in a showbag.'

A bag in a bag. I can't even begin to figure out how to refute her logic.

'If you think about it,' says Josh, surprising me with the optimism in his voice, 'we'll probably get twice as much stuff at the supermarket.'

I see the possibilities flash across Charlotte's face. Josh wipes the mucus from his nose onto his sleeve. It feels so strange and so warm having him on my side.

'I think we should go for it,' he says.

'What if we get in trouble for eating too much unhealthy stuff?' asks Charlotte.

'You won't get in trouble,' I say. 'I promise.'

'Alright, if you promise.'

I grab both of their hands and head towards the turnstiles. I don't want to give them time to change their minds. We pass the showbag pavilion and I still can't believe my luck. I'm actually looking forward to going shopping, racing home and spilling our bounty over the kitchen table. I'll let them stay up as late as they want and their tongues can turn blue from sucking on cheap sour straps. For now, thinking about their little blue tongues is enough. Just enough.

THE FIELDS
OF EARLY
SORROW

We encountered our first swarm of locusts on the flat, fertile plains approaching West Wyalong. Although the locusts splattered against the windscreen at great velocity, their demise was soundless. I was barely able to discern the white markings on the Newell Highway through the mass of smeared membranes. Acting on the advice of a cadet journalist who was raised in the region—in Bundaburrah, to be precise—I had secured aluminium mesh over the radiator to protect it. Katie sat sedately in the passenger seat and watched the locusts come to grief.

Once the threat of locusts had subsided, Katie wound the window down and lit a cigarette (I had bought her a carton of Marlboro Reds before we left). She tilted her head out the window while she smoked. It was only a small concession, but it filled my heart with warmth. Her dyed hair floated around her pale face. I caught sight of her auburn roots, which gleamed in the sun. Her complexion remained youthful, especially against the striking splash of her blue eyes. Her arms looked as slender as I could remember them looking since our adolescence.

Katie finished her cigarette and drew on a large pair of replica sunglasses. It was difficult to tell whether she was still awake after that. She had barely spoken all day. My wife, Pollyanna, had warned me that Katie might inexplicably lose her temper. She had also warned me not to invest too much faith in Katie's displays of good humour or kindness. It seemed strange to receive such solemn counsel regarding my younger sister, as though she was a criminal mastermind, waiting for an opening.

I followed the highway past quiet rural townships, rows of grapevines, fields of lavender, vast seeding machines, timber cattle yards and inviting weatherboard homesteads. The countryside looked resplendent in the afternoon sunlight. There wasn't another soul in sight. For a fleeting moment I forgot the circumstances of our journey and felt truly happy sitting behind the wheel. I dare say all happiness is fleeting. It is a great pity the same can't be said for sorrow.

I was forced to wait at a railway crossing on the outskirts of Forbes while a freight train approached. My gaze settled on a large plateau to the left of the highway that had been subdivided into paddocks. A flock of sheep was grazing the rich, volcanic soil. I wanted to wake Katie so she could share the view with me. But we weren't there to marvel at the landscape. It was this seemingly trivial act of suppression that caused me to feel disheartened for the first time all afternoon.

We still had several hours to drive to reach Dubbo. Pollyanna and I had decided that it was best to avoid stopping overnight in Sydney because there would be too many distractions. We would have another ten hours on the road the following day to get to the Buttery: a drug and alcohol clinic that was situated on three acres amid the rainforests and macadamia-nut plantations in the shire of Lismore. We had read numerous testimonials from ex-residents. One of them said he had found his soul again there. Katie had been on the waiting list for the past six months. In truth I was surprised she had made it.

I had taken one week of annual leave from my post as the editor-in-chief of the *Bendigo Advertiser*. I wondered whether the time would have been better spent taking my wife and my daughter to a beach resort up north somewhere. Having worked so diligently—I slept four hours per night on average—it seemed unfair to have to sacrifice a rare allotment of relaxation. I knew I couldn't burden Katie with my feelings, though. She already harboured enough guilt. Besides, driving her to the Buttery seemed like one of the few tasks that I had no right to delegate.

I frequently took note of Katie's features as she slept. She reminded me so much of my daughter, Ursula. While I had been loading Katie's belongings into the car that morning, Ursula ran into the street. She was wearing pink pyjamas. I had told Ursula that her aunty was taking a long holiday because she was feeling unwell. Ursula grabbed Katie around the waist and refused to let go. She said she hoped Katie would feel better when she got home so that they could hold tea parties in her cubbyhouse. Katie blinked several times. She wrapped her arms around Ursula's shoulders and kissed the child's flaxen hair.

■

Katie picked up a beer coaster and inspected the desolate bistro at the Parkes Leagues Club. Her pupils looked dilated in the bright lights. A group of young men were drinking beer at one of the nearby high tables. They had been playing pool when we first entered the building. I noticed one of them eyeing Katie off. She let out a high-pitched laugh.

'What's so funny?' I asked.

'I bet when we were children you never imagined you'd wind up in a place like this, guarding your kid sister like a prison warden.'

I didn't enjoy being likened to a prison warden. I felt that I had been quite good-natured about my responsibilities.

'You're right, it never crossed my mind.'

'Mine either,' she said.

A crowd of elderly people emerged through the glass doors, drowning out the bistro with genial murmur.

'But here we are,' said Katie.

'Yes, here we are.'

'And nothing in the world could persuade you to turn back.' It was difficult to gauge whether she was making a statement or asking a question.

'Nothing in the whole wide world,' I said.

Katie cast a sardonic smile at me. It wasn't the kind of smile a person wishes to behold in the eyes of a sibling.

'This must be very different to the hustle and bustle of a newsroom,' said Katie. She placed great emphasis on the words 'hustle' and 'bustle', as though they exemplified the difference between us; the thin metaphysical line between affliction and normality, or success.

'Obviously,' I said, trying to smile. 'I take solace in the fact that I don't have to worry about split infinitives in your presence.'

A waitress who walked with a pronounced limp brought our meals to the table. She inquired whether we were just passing through town.

'Yes,' I said. 'We're heading north.'

'Oh goody,' she said, clasping her hands together. She glanced at the mess that Katie was making with the beer coaster and turned to address me. 'Keep your eyes peeled for the big radio telescope twenty kilometres out of town. It's on the right side of the highway. The telescope was used to show man's first steps on the moon to the rest of the world.'

'We'll be sure not to miss it,' I said.

Katie thanked the waitress with a kindliness that sounded condescending.

I wasted no time in devouring my ribeye steak and soggy vegetables. I hadn't realised how hungry I was. We had only stopped three times all day: twice to fill up on petrol and once to buy sandwiches from a roadhouse in Deniliquin.

Katie barely touched her meal. I had ordered her a bowl of chicken and leek soup—one of the blackboard specials—without consulting her. No one had counselled me on what food she might find appealing.

'Are you ashamed of me?' she asked.

I was surprised that she posed the question in a public setting. She'd had all day to ask it while we were driving.

'No, I'm not ashamed of you.'

'Are you sure?'

'None of us are ashamed of you.'

Katie dabbed her spoon into her soup and watched the condensed liquid spill back into the bowl. 'Polly is ashamed of me,' she said. 'I can see it in the way she looks at me.'

'You're reading too much into everything. Pollyanna loves you the same as I do, the same as Ursula does. We all love you unconditionally. We just want you to get well again.'

'It's not that simple.'

'I know.'

Katie pushed her bowl into the middle of the table. She continued to clutch her spoon, in a bid to prevent her hand from shaking.

■

We found the Westview Caravan Park five kilometres out of Dubbo along the Mitchell Highway. Just prior to the turn-off, I noticed an abandoned drive-in that was bordered by a barbed-wire fence and rows of cactuses. We were greeted by a slim, affable man at the reception desk. He had slicked-back silver hair and wore a red flannelette shirt. As he was locating our booking in a hard-covered register, I asked him how long it had been since the drive-in was open.

'Must be almost twenty years now,' he said, pausing to suck on his bloodless lower lip. 'A man named Rex used to manage it. The crowds stopped coming, so I guess old Rex figured he ought to cut his losses. A man's got to read the signs.'

He swiped my credit card, glanced at the signature and handed it back.

'Most of the drive-ins in this country closed around that time. From memory the nearest one left is in the Hunter Valley. Awful pity, if you ask me. Mind you, Rex had a good run.'

He smiled at the ceiling and put the register away. He gave us directions to our cabin and asked us to return the key to his wife at reception by ten o'clock the next morning. I was relieved that he didn't inquire why we were passing through town.

Our cabin was in a sparsely populated lot in the heart of the caravan park. It was stifling inside. The blinds were drawn and the kitchenette had an acidic odour. I insisted that we both sleep in bunks in a small bedroom that was adjacent to the bathroom. I put my backpack on the bottom bed and unloaded a box of Corn Flakes and a carton of milk that I had purchased from a supermarket in town. Katie sat sullenly on a vinyl bench beside the fridge. She rubbed her shoes against the stained linoleum and complained that she was feeling nauseous.

Five minutes later I was reclining on a deckchair by the swimming pool, enjoying the shade of a palm tree. I was reading a copy of the *Daily Liberal*—a newspaper covering Dubbo and the surrounding district—which I had picked up at the reception desk. On the front page was a picture of a local wheat farmer. Dry skin was peeling off his nose. He had won the second-division prize in the national lottery. In spite of the six-figure windfall, he vowed to continue working on the family farm.

Katie removed her jeans and her blouse. She didn't have any bathers, so she had decided to swim in her underwear. Three young children—two boys and a girl who was wearing floaties around her arms—were playing in the shallow end of the pool. I guessed from their brazen familiarity with one another that they were siblings. The two boys briefly stopped teasing the girl when Katie entered the water. She waded to the deep end and lay on her back so that she could stare at the cloudless sky.

While I watched Katie float, I became aware that this allotment of time represented something vastly different to her. This time next week her wellbeing would no longer be in my control. She would be in the hands of strangers; people well versed in the realm of affliction, but still strangers. The swim was probably going to be her last allotment of peace for a while. This time next week I would be back sitting on a revolving chair in a newsroom, crosschecking citations, responding to readers' feedback and composing editorials, as though the scene at the swimming pool had never taken place.

Once more I began to contemplate the thin line between the poplars of an east-coast clinic and the brimming desks, the partitions, the air-conditioning units and the stark white lights of a newsroom. How had I managed to land on one side of the line while my sister landed on the other? Could the children playing in the swimming pool, splashing carelessly, conceive that their lives might take such a tumultuous course? Or was their bliss contingent upon the ignorance that such a course was possible?

■

The swimming pool was empty when I awoke. I returned to our cabin, expecting to find Katie asleep on the double mattress in the larger bedroom. She wasn't there. I followed a wide paved road and ended up running a frantic circuit of the caravan park. I searched the amenities block, even calling out Katie's name in the female toilets. No one answered. I saw a man in the communal barbecue area and ran up to him. He was filleting snapper. I tried to describe what Katie looked like as I was catching my breath. He raised his wet knife and pointed towards the Mitchell Highway.

I left the caravan park and jogged along the highway in the direction of town. The surrounding fields of canola had burst into dazzling displays of yellow. Several grain trucks rattled past. I had no idea why I had chosen to run in that direction or why it hadn't occurred to me to take the car. I knew that there was less than an hour of daylight remaining. The search would be hopeless once the sun had set. After following the highway for fifteen minutes, I decided to turn back.

When I had almost reached the caravan park I caught sight of a figure sitting in the middle of the abandoned drive-in. It was difficult to gain access to the property because of the rows of cactuses and the barbed-wire fence. I hurried past a rusted yellow-and-grey sign that read: WESTVIEW DRIVE-IN. Vegetation enveloped the old ticketing booth at the rear of the property.

I reached a side fence and called Katie's name. The figure looked in my direction, but made no obvious attempt to respond.

I took off my trousers and placed them over the barbed-wire. Once I had scaled it, I put them back on and ran through the knee-high rye grass. Katie was sitting facing the giant white screen. A herd of goats were grazing no more than twenty metres away. They didn't seem to mind her presence, or mine.

Katie's hands were smeared with blood. It was coming from a circular stain just below the ripped knee of her jeans. Her face looked frightfully pale.

'Do you think they'll give me something to dull the pain at the hospital?' she asked.

I tried not to smile.

Katie rolled up her jeans and inspected the wound on her right leg. It was deeper than I had expected. A crust of torn flesh was peeping out of a slit in her bloodied shin.

'Do you remember the first time we went to the drive-in?' she asked.

'You might have to refresh my memory.'

'Dad took us to see *Breaking Away*.'

'Now I remember,' I said, lowering myself gingerly to the grass. 'You were adamant that you were going to marry the lead actor. What was his name again?'

'Dennis Christopher.'

'Yes, you were rather smitten, as I recall.'

'Do you think I still have a chance?'

Crimson ripples bled into the distant sun, which had begun its descent behind the dark mountains on the horizon.

'Does your leg hurt?' I asked.

'I'll live,' said Katie. She ripped a wildflower from the soil and tucked it behind her ear. 'Although I'm not sure how I feel about that.'

'You won't be able to poach Mister Christopher from beyond the grave,' I said, attempting to be funny.

'The main memory I have of the film is that scene at the quarry where the four boys are lying with their shirts off. I can't remember the last time I felt so happy.'

I still felt happiness on a daily basis: at the sight of Ursula wearing her pink pyjamas in the morning, for instance.

'Do you think I'll ever experience it again?'

'It's not for me to say.'

'But if I'm not going to experience it again, what's the point in any of this? Isn't life supposed to be the pursuit of happiness?'

'I don't think it's supposed to be anything.'

'All I know is I'm sick of feeling ashamed all the time. I've endured enough shame for one lifetime. Even the small moments of happiness I can remember from the past seem worthless compared to the density of this feeling. There's no respite, not for me.' She exhaled sharply and shook her head. 'I don't even believe in a soul.'

I considered hugging her, but I suspected that the gesture would be insufficient. We didn't hug often enough.

'When you get home I'd like you to do me a favour.'

'Anything,' I said.

Katie inspected her right leg. Blood continued to trickle down her shin, staining her socks.

'I'd like you to tell Ursula the truth.'

'She won't understand.'

'That's not important.'

A warm northerly swept across the rye grass. Ironbarks twitched in the distance. My gaze settled on the towering blank screen. White paint was beginning to peel away from its surface.

WHEN THERE'S
NOWHERE ELSE
TO RUN

My turn by Jenna's bedside started at eight o'clock in the morning. She slept the whole time. I talked to her anyway. I knew from work that hearing was always one of the last senses to go. The first few times she slept I couldn't think of what to say, but then I started telling her things that I hadn't talked to anyone else about. It was actually quite liberating. I spent most of the morning talking to her about the private girls school I had attended back home in Johannesburg. Then I told her about our family's old maid, Wanda, because she was in no state to judge me.

Afterwards I saw Ben sitting out on the decking, staring at the red gums. He was holding the previous week's Green Guide. I was glad Jenna would never see him like that. He wouldn't have let her. He smiled at me in that pained way he had learnt over the past two years. It seemed unimaginable that he'd once drunkenly chased her around the living room of our share house with a couch pillow between his teeth, growling and barking. I remembered her screaming, 'Stop it, Ben! I'm serious, fucking stop it or we're through!' But he didn't stop it and they weren't through.

I told him I was taking a walk into town and he was welcome to join me.

'No thanks,' he said. 'I'm okay.'

We'd made a point of giving Ben space and not asking how he was feeling. It was easy to see how he was feeling.

'Come on, we don't even have to talk,' I said. 'It's a nice walk, trust me.'

He put down the Green Guide.

We walked downhill in silence until we reached the town. I bought two takeaway coffees from an upmarket café on the foreshore. There were flyers up all over town for a model boat regatta the following weekend. I decided that I'd wander down to watch it if we were still around. We continued walking past an open-water swimming pool and the surf lifesaving club. Grey clouds were rolling in above the mountains. We sat on the sand and stared at a handful of surfers who were trying to catch waves in the bay.

'When it's over I think I'll go overseas for a year or two,' said Ben.

'Anywhere in particular?'

'No, I haven't really thought about where. I'll come back eventually. I just need some time alone.' He scratched his messy hair.

'Twenty-seven isn't fair,' he said. 'Or it doesn't seem fair. I know heaps of people don't even get to live that long. People in third world countries, I mean. But on these shores it feels like an injustice.'

In the past few weeks I'd regularly had the same thought.

'All that study and all those good grades and all our planning for a future that was never going to happen. It seems kind of pointless now. I know that's the wrong way to think about it. It's just, I keep thinking maybe if we'd known everything right from the start, we would have done things differently.'

I wanted to say that he didn't have to do this to himself, but since he was finally speaking, I decided to leave it alone.

'Sorry,' he said, watching a surfer miss a wave. 'How do you feel about it all?'

'I think I'm still assembling my feelings, or trying to. For now all I know is that we have to be there for her and nothing else, but not to pretend like it's not happening when we're with her, if that makes any sense. I hope she can't tell how scared I am. Because if I'm scared, I don't know how scared she might be.'

'I don't think she's scared at all, you know. It feels like she's beyond that. Being scared implies there's hope, and there's no hope anymore.'

I wondered whether Ben would ever come back if he went overseas.

'I think I'll keep walking,' he said.

He stood up, brushed the sand off his jeans and set off along the beach. When he was halfway to the jetty, he turned around and walked back to me. He poured several moist coins into my hand.

'That's for the coffee. Sorry, I almost forgot.'

■

When I got back, there was a delicious aroma throughout the house. A bolognese sauce was simmering on the stovetop. Maurice and Frank were slouched in the open-plan living room, watching an Owen Wilson comedy. Frank was the only person who'd thought to bring DVDs. Jenna hated his taste in movies. She couldn't believe they had both come from the same womb. Unlike Frank, she liked movies and shows that actually gave the viewer a bit of credit. When we lived together, we used to pirate HBO shows and churn through them in our pyjamas. One time we almost got through two series of *The Wire* in a day.

I sat on the sofa and pulled my sleeping bag over my shoulders, quickly slipping out of consciousness. Every so often my head would jolt forwards and my eyes would struggle to focus on the plasma screen. It would take a few seconds of blinking before

I remembered where I was and why I was there. My heart must have broken six or seven times.

Maurice woke me when lunch was ready. The television had been switched off.

'We've all got to eat,' he said.

I joined Frank at the table. Ben still hadn't returned from his walk. I wasn't worried. Walking was just about the best thing he could be doing. Maurice put the remaining bowls of pasta in the fridge and joined us. Frank stood up and raised his plastic cup of red wine. Even though Ben had given us the go-ahead to plough through the contents of his cellar, I knew the sight of Frank with that plastic cup would still have given him a heart attack.

'To staying strong,' said Frank.

We ate in silence for several minutes.

'Maurice, I think this might be the nicest meal I've ever eaten,' I said.

'Fresh pasta,' he said, taking another mouthful of wine.

We ate on in silence as the wind buffeted the retractable glass doors. It was a lovely house. Frank's girlfriend, Megan, had found it online. The owners were super friendly about the situation. They'd cancelled all bookings for the next month and told us that we could sort out a price at the other end. I had no idea how my life was going to function again at the other end.

When I tuned back in to the conversation, Frank was telling Maurice about a man in his office who took several fifteen-minute bathroom breaks every morning. He and some of his colleagues had started a secret spreadsheet to record the man's bowel movements. Maurice was laughing and I found myself laughing too. It felt nice. Frank was good like that, although I still hated it when he mocked my accent. He sounded more like a New Zealander. Jenna always described him to strangers as a big, loveable oaf. There weren't any other words for him.

Megan appeared in the living room, mascara running down her cheeks. Frank stopped talking about the spreadsheet and gave her a big hug. Maurice rinsed his bowl and made his way to the master bedroom. Even though it had been over five years, it must have been strange for him. I still remembered what Jenna had said when they first started going out. The sex wasn't great, she'd confided. When she'd finally ended it, she told me, 'He's just too nice.' Somehow, with age, 'nice' seemed like less of a deterrent.

■

Ben returned just before nightfall. Megan offered to heat up some pasta for him, but he said he wasn't hungry. He curled up on the sofa and fell asleep. I watched him wincing and turning restlessly. It was sad seeing him use a pillow for its intended purpose instead of putting it between his teeth and growling.

I was sitting in the cafeteria at the hospital when he'd called to break the news. I'd just finished a night shift. His delivery was painfully dry. He had already spoken to Frank and Jenna's parents, he told me, his voice eerily measured and calm. It seemed awful that he'd had to invent a protocol for the call. Afterwards I sat in the empty cafeteria and imagined him making a list of friends and their phone numbers, coming up with a script to help him get through each call without falling apart. Now, as I watched the violence of his sleep, I realised that he was still trying to postpone the falling-apart.

'Should we do the dishes?' I whispered to Megan.

'Yeah, great idea.'

I piled the dishes into the sink and ran some hot water. Megan and I had come to look forward to the ritual, even though the house had a state-of-the-art dishwasher.

'Frank was hilarious at lunch today,' I said.

'He wasn't talking about the spreadsheet, was he?'

We both laughed.

'I think the whole thing's awful,' she said. 'Imagine how bad the guy's going to feel if he finds out. I love him, but Frank's not exactly discreet.'

I started rinsing the plastic cups. 'So,' I said.

'So,' she sighed, without any of her usual bubbliness. It was strange to see Megan looking so uncertain. During our first few days at the house, she kept calling me into the bedroom to make sure everything was okay. She reminded me of the anxious relatives I often had to deal with at work.

'It sounded like she was gurgling a bit today,' she said.

'Don't worry,' I said. 'That's normal. She doesn't have a strong enough cough reflex to get rid of all the mucus and saliva that's building up.'

'Are you sure she's not in much pain?'

'Yeah, I'm sure.'

I watched her absently colour-coordinating the plastic cups on a tea towel. 'Do you remember the Blues and Roots Festival?' she asked. 'That's about as loose as I've ever seen her.'

I smiled. I hadn't thought about the Blues and Roots Festival in ages. I remembered the night that Jenna and Ben dropped a tab of acid each before a George Clinton set. They wound up having a naked dip at the beach. It certainly made me feel like a private-school girl. Afterwards she returned to our tent at the Arts Factory, shivering, and asked if I could hold her until she felt normal again.

'She told me if she let go of the lip balm in her left hand, she was going to go into cardiac arrest,' I said.

'What?' said Megan, smiling.

'I know. I tried to calm her down with some basic medical facts, but she still wouldn't let go of it.' It felt like we were already starting to talk about her in the past tense.

I noticed that Ben had joined Maurice out on the decking. They were passing a joint back and forth, both staring into the blustery evening.

'Frank said she wants me to play at the funeral,' said Megan, removing a stack of forks from the dish rack and drying them one at a time.

'Do you think you'll be up to it?' I asked.

'I don't know. How can you tell?'

'I guess you can't.'

'I'm starting to get a bit worried about it,' she said. 'I've never been to a funeral that wasn't for a family pet.'

■

The curtains were open, allowing a dark purplish light to wash into the master bedroom. I crawled into the bed and lay next to Jenna. Ben had replaced the sheets and covered her feet with woollen socks. Her lips looked dry and sore. It had been over a week since I'd told everyone they weren't allowed to put small ice cubes in her mouth anymore. I inspected her engagement ring. Her fingers felt like chalk that might snap if I pressed too firmly. I felt the portacath that jutted out below her collarbone. At first the strange contraption had frightened the others. Frank said it looked like something out of *Dawn of the Dead*.

I lay there for almost an hour, watching her and listening to her breathing. It started to sound less regular, so I propped another small pillow under her head. I studied her hollowed-out cheeks. They seemed so dreadfully incapable of laughter. Jenna laughed more than any person I'd ever met, even more than

Frank. I took some solace from the fact that even if I lived for another fifty or sixty years, she would still have laughed more than me.

I sat up in the bed and started to tell her about a man I'd dated the previous month. We'd met on a Friday night when I was out drinking with some of the younger nurses. He was a member of the metropolitan fire brigade. He explained how the wet pipe sprinkler system worked at the bar we were drinking at. Aside from that, he seemed normal. We both worked crazy hours. The next week we went to a Moroccan soup bar and ended up back at my place. Once we got beneath the covers, he burst into tears and started telling me how he'd just lost custody of his twin daughters.

'Why do I always attract men like that?' I asked out loud. I knew Jenna would have had a field day with it. It felt surprisingly normal telling her about my dating woes, even though I knew they were trivial compared to her suffering. She had taken it with such grace from the beginning, fighting when there was a fight to be had and understanding when the fight's outcome was decided. She never seemed scared. The hardest part at work was when they were afraid right up until the end.

There were still so many things I wanted to know, questions I had wanted to ask but had never quite found the right moment for. What was it like when no one else was around? Did she view it as an injustice? Did she want to scream 'why me?' a thousand times over? I already knew that no matter what good came my way in life, there would always be a part of me that would resent this and view it as proof of an almighty failure.

I knew we'd never speak again. It had been days since she'd given any sign of knowing who I was. One of the last times we'd had a proper conversation was when we were driving along the Great Ocean Road on the way to the house. Ben thought it would be nice for her to see the coastline. I'd sat in the back with her and we'd talked about our favourite stand-up comedians. I tried to do Trevor Noah's impersonation of the South African president. As we were approaching the Twelve Apostles, Jenna asked me to wind down the window. She wanted to feel the wind from the Southern Ocean on her face. 'That feels so nice,' she said, eyes half-closed. 'Thanks for everything.'

■

I woke up in Frank's gymnasium-built arms as he was carrying me back out to the living room. First light was breaking over the bay. I could see Maurice's silhouette on the decking, so I made a cup of tea and joined him outside. He offered to roll a joint, but I declined. The tag was hanging out the neck of his grey Kmart jumper. It had been days since he'd changed clothes.

'Have you been to sleep yet?' I asked.

'I haven't really felt like it.'

'How are you feeling?'

'Not bad.' He removed a tissue of skin from his lips. 'Those loose veins on her hands freak me out,' he said. 'I don't know how you put up with it every day.'

'People often say stuff like that to me. It's weird, you kind of get used to it. Or you learn to build up a bit of a wall between yourself and the patients. Sometimes it all catches up with you at the end of a shift. I know a few of the girls are on Ativan.'

'Do you have a wall with her?'

'No, that's the hard part. I'm too invested. She's the last person in the world I ever wanted to treat as a patient. Maybe it seems like I'm in control. I don't know.'

'It does seem like you're in control,' he said. 'We all feel safer when you're in there with her.'

The bay looked calm. I doubted that I'd get to attend the model boat regatta.

'So, how long were you up north for?' I asked.

'About half a year. It was a good piece of escapism, wasn't it?' He smiled sheepishly. 'She said we were better off as friends. It was a bit patronising, but when I see her around Ben, I know she's right.'

I liked that he was still talking about her in the present tense.

'What was it like up there?' I asked.

'It was exactly what I needed. My uncle owns a seafood restaurant in Bundaberg, so he put me up and gave me some hours in the kitchen. I started out washing dishes, then worked my way up to doing some food prep. That's how I sort of fell into cooking.' He wiped his nose with his sleeve. 'It's not very glamorous or anything.'

'We've all got to eat.' I hoped I didn't sound patronising.

'I suppose I just liked the routines. I remember mopping the floor at the end of every shift and hosing the mats and the milk crates down in the break area, knowing I was getting everything ready for the next morning. Sometimes it's nice to simplify everything. It helped take my mind off her, sort of like finding a way back to zero.'

'See?' I said. 'I'd rather wait on sick people than work in a sweaty kitchen all day.'

He smiled and rubbed his sparse facial hair. 'I tell you what,' he said, rising from the decking. 'Why don't we make some breakfast for everyone?'

'Sure.'

We made our way quietly to the kitchen. Frank and Megan were asleep on the sofa, which was strange, because it was supposed to be Megan's turn to sit with Jenna. Maurice inspected the pantry. It was getting pretty bare. He removed a bottle of milk and half a carton of eggs from the fridge.

'How about pancakes?' he asked.

'Sounds perfect.'

He handed me the milk and the eggs and started rummaging around in the cupboards. 'I'll see if I can track down a jug for you to whisk them in,' he said. 'They've got pancakes in Africa, right?'

'No, we only eat lions and giraffes and zebras.'

'That's a pity.'

He found a jug for me. I cracked an egg into it as he started sifting flour into a large mixing bowl.

'When you're done, pour that mixture into the bowl,' he said. 'Please.'

I grinned as we exchanged glances, feeling stupidly guilty because I was starting to enjoy myself.

■

Ben walked into the living room while the rest of us were watching an action movie that was full of tedious car chases. He made eye contact with me and tilted his head. I followed him into the master bedroom, my heart racing. Sunlight was punching into the room through the window, accentuating the pallor of Jenna's face. I knelt down beside the bed, but I already knew. I checked for a pulse, nodded at Ben and told him I was sorry. He opened the window and tucked her arm back underneath the covers.

We returned to the living room. The others could tell as soon as they looked at Ben. Without speaking, we gathered around and hugged him. Megan's eyes were brimming with tears. She grabbed a box of tissues from the coffee table and blew her nose. Frank walked out to the decking, clutched the railing and looked out over the bay. Maurice joined him. I didn't know what I was supposed to do anymore. I paused the action movie. It all seemed kind of hopeless without her. I'd tried to avoid thinking about what it would feel like. Now that it had finally arrived, my grief felt endless.

Ben walked over to the television, removed the movie and slotted a new disc into the DVD player. He studied the remote control and pointed it at the absurdly large screen, increasing the volume until the floorboards were reverberating. I heard the familiar dripping of keys at the beginning of the song and then Brandon Flowers started crooning like a heartthrob. Jenna was always a sucker for The Killers. It was about as mainstream as she got. One time I tried telling her that her boy Brandon was a Mormon, but she'd just grinned and said, 'I'm happy to convert for him.'

Frank came in from outside and wiped Megan's eyes with his fat thumbs. He kissed her hair, tucked her used tissues into his pockets and started twirling her awkwardly around to the music. He couldn't dance to save himself. Six foot three of oaf. He released Megan so that he could clench his fists and belt out a hoarse, tone-deaf chorus.

Ben started shuffling behind the sofa with his eyes closed. It had been years since I'd seen him dance. Megan was rocking her hips from side to side and swaying her head to the bassline.

She couldn't look ugly if she tried. I remembered when the three of us went to see The Killers at the showgrounds on Jenna's twenty-fourth birthday. We'd danced for two hours straight that night. This was a different dance. I wasn't conscious of being prompted by any particular instrument or sound. I just let my limbs flail and my body do whatever it needed to.

Maurice joined us during the breakdown in the middle of the song, mouthing the lyrics and wriggling his bony shoulders, sweating like he was working in a busy kitchen. He looked like he was trying to shimmy the mothballs out of his jumper. I wondered whether he'd learnt any country moves in Bundaberg. It didn't look like it. His elbows were wobbling about and he was grimacing, or maybe smiling. He met my gaze, bleary-eyed, and offered his right hand. I reached out and took hold of it.

THE LAST TROUT
THAT RICHARD
BOUGHT FOR ALICE

Richard snakes through the narrow backstreets of Brunswick in his old Subaru, trying to avoid the late afternoon traffic. He stops at a roundabout to let three kids in blue uniforms cross the street. It's funny. Up until a few years ago, when he met Alice, he couldn't see himself having kids. But now he can't think of anything nicer than finishing his run for the day and picking up a few youngsters from school, still wearing his Australia Post uniform, maybe stopping at a milk bar to buy Calippos if it's stinking hot.

As he's approaching a futon store near Barkly Square, he catches sight of an unmistakably lanky figure from his university days, back when he fancied himself as a painter. He pulls over.

'Wes!' he calls out, winding down the passenger window.

The lanky figure looks around in a bit of a daze, before finally noticing him.

'Richard,' says Wes, grinning clumsily. 'Long time, no see.' He's wearing a flannelette shirt that's a couple of sizes too big, giving him an uncanny resemblance to a scarecrow.

'Listen,' says Wes, glancing into the distance. 'I hate to ask, but I'm a bit pressed for time. Any chance of a quick lift to the Edinburgh Castle?'

'Sure,' says Richard. 'Hop in.'

Wes has to tuck his knees up to fit into the front seat. Richard swings the car around and turns right onto Sydney Road. He gets stuck behind a tram straight away. As they wait, he wonders whether he'd make better headway riding along the footpath on his little Honda, stopping at letterboxes every five or ten metres.

'Still painting?' he asks, smelling turpentine.

'Trying to,' says Wes, scouting the crowd outside the Penny Black, who seem to get younger every week. 'Hey, want to grab a feed with us and play some ping pong?'

'I can't,' says Richard. 'My girlfriend's students are putting on a show tonight. I've got to be there in half an hour.'

'Maybe next time,' says Wes, unbuckling his seatbelt.

He ruffles Richard's hair before getting out at the next traffic light. Richard watches through the window as Wes walks into the pub and leans against the horseshoe bar next to a few regulars, probably waiting for some tattooed rockabilly woman to serve him.

When the lights go green, Richard turns left, but he gets stuck at the level crossing at Anstey Station. The gates stay down for several minutes, even though there's no sign of any train coming. At least a hundred cars could've driven through by now. It was a mistake taking Albion Street. He winds down his window and lets the crisp scent of Lebanese bread seep into the car, but his eyes still wander to the clock on the dashboard. Alice is probably waiting in the foyer of the Flemington Community Centre already, making small talk with colleagues. The last thing he wants is to have to sneak into the performance late and sit separately to her.

One of the cars on the other side of the crossing swerves onto the wrong side of the road and drives around the boom gates. No one beeps at them. Another two cars quickly follow suit. Richard reverses about a metre, which gives him just enough room to squeeze past the hatchback in front of him. When he reaches the gates, he slows down to survey the tracks. No trains coming. As he accelerates through the crossing, he feels the exhilaration spread through his body, and just like that, he's through.

The evening sun pours over the brick-veneer houses, giving the street a sharp orange glow. He reaches up to adjust the sun visor, but something appears out of nowhere behind the tray of a parked ute, leaving him no time to hit the brakes or veer out of its way. He hears his toolkit shift in the back seat. There's a thud as a heavy form collides with his bonnet and then its skull crashes into his windscreen, cracking it like a spider's web.

■

Richard keeps driving downhill, past a rundown playground, over the tollway, towards the Moonee Valley racecourse. The left side of his windscreen is spattered with blood. It's a fact. He knows any decent person would've stopped straight away. Every second is making it worse. But he already feels helpless to arrest this worsening, this constricting of time. The further he drives, the less he feels like turning around and facing up to whatever it is that he's just done.

It wasn't his fault, he's certain of that much. But he knows that if he goes back now, no one's going to believe him, especially since he skipped the crossing. All the questions he'll have to answer and all the holes they'll find in his story. He doesn't even have a clue what his story is. What actually happened back there? One second he was driving and the next someone appeared out of nowhere. It was all so fast. The only thing he maybe shouldn't have done is reach for the sun visor, but it wouldn't have changed anything.

There's no way he can get away with it, is there? No, surely there were witnesses. There were dozens of cars banked up on the opposite side of the street. By now there's probably an ambulance on the scene and it won't be long until people are reciting his number plates to stone-faced policemen. Plus there'll be CCTV footage. Is anyone following him? No, good. No helicopters overhead, either. What he really needs now is time to figure out how he's going to explain it all, word by word. If he can just get his story straight, there might be a chance that they'll believe him.

He parks his car in a residential street near the racetrack; when he gets out he instinctively notes that he's parked in a permit zone. Not that it matters. There's a huge dent in the bonnet and a large smear of something on his right windscreen wiper. Membrane of some kind. He searches in the boot for a rag to wipe it off with, but he realises that he'll never be able to get every last trace of it off the car. Besides, what can he really do about the bonnet and the windscreen? No mechanic is going to agree to keep it a secret, at least none he'll ever be able to find.

He pulls a Phillips head screwdriver out of his toolkit and starts unscrewing his front number plate. It's calming, in a way, watching the cross-shaped screw heads slowly come loose. Once he's removed all the screws from both number plates, he peels his registration sticker away from the inside of the windscreen and stows it in his toolkit. He dumps his belongings in the first rubbish bin he sees and walks towards Mount Alexander Road, staring at the empty grandstands overlooking the racetrack. The grass in the straight is immaculate and the flowers will still bloom in spring. He just isn't sure whether he'll be around to see them.

A tram approaches within seconds and a group of kids with school bags spill out of the front carriage, drinking Slurpees and laughing. One of them brushes against Richard's shoulder and he feels a wave of indignation rise up in his chest. He just manages to refrain from throttling the little prick, instead boarding the tram and negotiating the aisle. No one even glances at him. There's a vacant booth at the rear of the second carriage. It reeks of deodorant. He sits down and drops his head into his hands, trying to figure out what on earth he's going to say to Alice.

■

Alice is leaning against the side of the Flemington Community Centre, wearing a yellow dress that Richard loves. When she recognises him, she gives him a quick hug and kisses him on the neck.

'You're lucky we're on African time,' she says, smiling.

'Sorry,' he says. 'I ended up catching the tram.'

'Come on, let's head inside.' She grabs his hand and leads him hurriedly towards the entrance. Richard really just wants to stay outside in the fresh air and confess, but he can't bring himself to resist her. The foyer is crowded with murmuring people whom he half expects to turn around and stare at him in disgust.

'Thanks so much for coming,' says Alice, fixing the side part of his hair. 'Tell me about your day.'

His face is almost too stiff to speak. 'It's a bit complicated,' he says, feeling his heart suddenly racing.

'That's alright, it looks like we've got time.'

Richard breathes in and exhales slowly, but it doesn't help. It all seemed so much simpler when he was rehearsing it in his head on the tram.

'Hi, Miss Alice,' says a curvy girl in a bright green hijab, walking towards them.

'Rahama,' says Alice, smiling warmly. 'It's lovely to see you.'

Rahama glances at Richard's uniform as though there's something strange on it. Is there a fleck of blood he's missed? 'Hi, Mister Alice,' she says, giggling into her hand.

'Nice to meet you,' he manages to say.

'Rahama's in my year ten ESL class,' says Alice to Richard.

He has the feeling that he ought to be saying something or asking something, but he can't think what it is.

'Anyway,' says Rahama, looking only at Alice now, 'I hope you like the show.'

'Good luck, sweetie.'

They join a line outside the auditorium that's moving at a snail's pace. Richard wishes he could just sit down. How long is it going to take for them to find him? They won't come in halfway through the performance to take him away, will they? Not that it'll make much of a difference. All he wishes is that he could live the last hour of his life over again. He envies everyone in the crowded foyer. There's not a single person that he wouldn't trade places with in a heartbeat.

'Richie,' says Alice, waving her hand in front of his eyes. 'Are you alright?'

He tries to nod the way he usually would.

'You look really pale. Why don't you quickly go and splash some water on your face?'

'I'm fine, seriously.'

He notices with relief that they're at the entrance to the auditorium. Prams spill into the aisles and young children are kneeling on the floorboards near the stage, jostling for position in front of the speakers. Richard recognises some of Alice's old students. There's Abdi with the long braids. Priscilla in the Lakers singlet. Omar with his cap on sideways. He's put on heaps of weight. A hunched man with long hair gets up on stage to introduce the performance.

'And it all begins with a huge round of applause from you!' he cries at the end of his speech, and Richard watches, motionless, as the audience breaks into applause.

The performance starts with a halal pizza delivery boy being extradited to his country of birth in Africa. The immigration officials are played as fat, slapstick characters, drawing loud laughter from the audience. Richard watches Alice laughing her perfect laugh. He knows it's too late to tell her now and that this will be the last performance by her students that he ever gets to see. And he knows he'll never wake up at the crack of dawn to sort through his mail trays again, he'll never get to check the tyre pressure on his Honda, he'll never get to whisper to Alice's swollen belly like they've joked about or help blow out the candles on a child's birthday cake.

■

Alice is opening another bottle of cheap shiraz and singing a Sharon Jones song in the kitchen, but she doesn't quite have the pipes for it. Richard, still disconcertingly sober, can feel the vibrations of a late-night tram through the bedframe. He stares at an old oil painting of Wes's that's hanging on the bedroom wall. It's of a sea of nutshells on the tiles beside leather shoes in a Spanish pinchos bar. Wes named the painting *El Clásico*.

It's strange, Richard feels like he's never really looked at the painting properly until now. The brushwork on the nutshells is so subtle and he loves the way the natural light intersects with the leather shoes. Then there's the way that Wes has blended the grout between the tiles into the shadows of some of the nutshells.

Alice returns to the bedroom with two topped-up glasses, still singing. Richard is surprised by the click in his blood at the sight of her.

'Rahama was hilarious tonight, wasn't she?' says Alice, handing him the glass.

'Yep,' he says, swallowing. 'She's a real natural on stage.'

'I know. It's so nice to see her up there enjoying herself. Her family spent three years in a refugee camp in Kenya. I can't imagine how that must've been.'

It's the last thing he really wants to think about.

'I told her I'd fast again this year, for Ramadan,' says Alice, settling on the bed. 'She was really excited.'

'Great,' says Richard, trying to force a smile. He remembers Alice waking up before sunrise last winter, drinking two litres of water every morning and loading up on carbohydrates.

'Also, I forgot to ask,' says Alice, her cheeks flushed. 'What happened to your car?'

'Sorry, what?' asks Richard, his chest throbbing.

'I thought you said you caught the tram, so where's the car?'

He has a long drink. 'I ended up leaving it near the racetrack,' he says, not wanting to lie to her. 'The traffic was awful. I think there must have been an accident or something.'

'So when are you going to pick it up?' she asks, putting on a sweet young girl's voice that usually drives him crazy with desire.

'Sometime tomorrow, I guess.'

'Okay,' says Alice, dropping the voice and folding her legs so that her dress creeps up her thin, pale thighs. 'Stop being so uptight, you're making me feel funny.'

'Sorry.'

'You should be.'

He swallows the rest of his shiraz, wishing he could at least start feeling tipsy.

'You're very cute,' she says, resting her glass on the bedside table. 'Do you know that?'

'I should water the herbs,' he says, suddenly sitting upright. 'It's been a few days.'

'What? Why don't you just do it in the morning?' She neatens his hair and kisses him. 'You okay?'

'Fine.'

She kisses him again, this time biting his lower lip playfully until he withdraws.

'I might as well do it while I still remember,' he says, trying to make it sound like the most rational thing in the world.

'Okay,' she says, sighing. 'If you have to.'

Richard walks out to the balcony and kneels down, steadying his breathing as he pokes around the dry soil in the vertical herb garden. Another tram rattles past. He tips water into the patch where the coriander and the parsley are growing, watching it soak into the soil, knowing the leaves will be ready in a couple of weeks.

■

Richard lies in bed, listening to Alice's oblivious breathing, still waiting for a knock at the front door. At 2 am he switches on the clock radio so that he can listen to the news headlines. He braces himself as he hears the orchestral build-up at the start of the ABC bulletin. The female newsreader's nasal voice sounds so impassive. Why can't they just talk like normal people? She makes no mention of an accident in Brunswick or a blood-spattered Subaru found near the racetrack, leaving him feeling almost disappointed.

He brushes the cobwebs off Alice's bicycle and sets off through the local streets. It feels great getting back out on a bike, especially without being weighed down by twenty kilos of mailbags. He's all over the road at first, but he eventually gets used to the high handlebars. He picks up speed on Lygon Street and flies past the Red Wheelbarrow, Alice's favourite second-hand bookshop, where they often browse on Saturday mornings before doing their weekly shop at the market.

Realising he's starving, Richard stops at an all-night kebab caravan out the front of a carwash on Sydney Road. As he waits behind a couple of glazed-eyed teenagers, he starts feeling guilty for having an appetite. One of the teenagers wrestles the other into a headlock and starts cackling. Richard hopes that whoever it was he hit doesn't have children. But they are, or were, someone's child. There's probably already weeping. Somewhere in the city a house is filling with grief and he has filled it. Maybe relatives have already started baking. *I am a decent person*, he wishes he could tell them.

Once his lamb kebab is ready, he moves to the courtyard outside the Mechanics Institute and watches the traffic go by, savouring the overpowering taste of the garlic sauce. A handful of people are smoking at the tables that spill into the street outside the Retreat, where grainy soul music is coming from. They're all laughing about something. He hears the deafening splutter of motorbikes approaching and then speeding off towards the city, strangling the night.

A tall man stands up from one of the nearby tables and staggers across the intersection, forcing several cars to wait at the traffic lights, before eventually managing to hail a taxi out the front of the town hall. For a second Richard could swear that it's Wes, but the posture isn't quite right. He watches until the taxi disappears from sight. If he'd just not seen Wes in the first place, or not pulled over and given him a lift, or if the bloody person hadn't emerged out of nowhere without even checking for oncoming traffic, both of them would still be fine. It was peak hour, for Christ's sake. What kind of idiot just runs out into a busy street like that?

He finishes his kebab and mounts the bicycle, pedalling out into the middle of Sydney Road. It's invigorating having the tram tracks to himself. The men inside Café Coco are still watching football and smoking hookahs. He catches a whiff of apple shisha. Alice is always saying how the smell reminds her of the streets of Cairo, not that he's ever been. Not that he'll ever get to go with her now.

He loves this hectic suburb with its coffee roasting houses, overpriced bars, cafés in old weighbridges, fabric emporiums, bridal salons, Mediterranean wholesalers, halal butchers, rotting pallets and abandoned factories. A year ago two men were gunned down at a nearby panelbeaters in broad daylight. The address was on Richard's daily run. He remembers how he felt when he realised that; how he secretly loved the feeling of being so close to the action, yet so far away from it.

■

Even though it's barely 6 am, the butchers at the Queen Victoria Market are already spruiking in the aisles, hands tucked into their armpits. Richard feels safe among the growing crowd in the meat and fish hall, cradling a cardboard crate. It's much harder shopping without Alice, but he wants to fill the fridge and the pantry with everything that she loves. Asparagus. Fruit and nut bread. Cheeses. Freshly ground coffee.

'We'll take two dollars off mid-loin lamb chops, have a look at the quality!' hollers a butcher with a lopsided nose, trying to fix eyes with Richard.

Richard avoids him by studying the steel rails where the butchers hang animal carcasses and push them around to their stalls first thing in the morning. He feels a great affinity for these men and women who will continue to inhabit the early hours of the morning, which is indisputably the greatest time of day to be alive.

He waits in line at a seafood outlet near the city entrance, staring at the vaulted ceilings, the dim blue lights, the fillets of salmon and the empty eyes of the trout resting on beds of ice. The eyes need to be empty, not cloudy. Richard's favourite fishmonger has explained it to him countless times. When he reaches the front of the line, the fishmonger grins with his bloodshot eyes.

'Where's your beautiful lady?' asks the fishmonger, his voice already hoarse.

Richard hesitates, feeling a sudden wave of exhaustion. For the life of him, he can't think of anything witty to say. 'She's still sleeping.'

'Ah, now I see who wears the pants.' The fishmonger grins again, eyes ablaze.

Richard finally remembers something about him and feels a rush of relief. 'How do you think the Blues will go this year?' he asks.

'Ah, she's not going to be pretty,' says the fishmonger, wincing. 'If you ask me, the players aren't up to it.'

'What about the coach?'

'Never mind him. It doesn't matter who the coach is. It's the players. They don't bleed for the cause. That's the real problem. These days they get paid all that money and they've got none of *this*,' says the fishmonger, thumping the chest of his apron.

'I know what you mean,' says Richard.

'Sometimes I wonder what we're actually paying them for. The members, I mean. Imagine if I tried to do this job with no ticker, do you think I'd make a living?'

'I guess not.'

'Exactly. How do you think I feel when I pay my membership fees and my kids' membership fees and I see no heart? After a while it seems like a kick in the teeth to me, you know.'

Richard nods and points at a fish with bright red gills behind the glass. 'I'll have that one, please.'

The fishmonger slides it into a plastic bag, handling the fish with an intimacy that seems both stern and tender. He weighs it on the scales then wraps the plastic bag in butcher's paper, glancing back up at Richard. 'I'd play for free, you know, if they asked me to.'

Richard laughs. Almost eleven dollars, he sees the fish is going to cost, but it doesn't matter because seafood is Alice's favourite.

'No, I'm serious,' says the fishmonger, handing Richard the package and speaking more emphatically. 'I'd play for free. Honest to God. Just to show them what it's all about. You can't buy heart, my friend, not human heart anyway.'

Richard tries to keep laughing as he reaches into his wallet, because he wants to make sure he enjoys the fishmonger's convictions about football, however fanciful, one last time.

QUEEN
ADELAIDE
RESTAURANT

Knuckles rapped against the door to my compartment. I was lying on the foldout bed, reading.

'Good morning in there.'

I recognised the soft inflection of the young stewardess who had been assigned to my carriage. I didn't respond. She turned the handle and pushed the door ajar, revealing the slender fingers on her right hand.

'Tell me, does anyone sleep a wink on the Indian Pacific?' I asked.

'Actually, it's the opposite for me,' she said, poking her head around the door and smiling. 'I've done the trip so many times now that I find it harder to sleep on a still bed.'

'That's incredible,' I said, wanting to keep the conversation going.

'Breakfast's in ten minutes,' she said, closing the door.

I took a photograph through the window. The clouds that had obscured the rising sun had finally dispersed. A number of small pools lined the karst terrain beside the tracks, reflecting the blue sky back at itself.

I buttoned up the same cotton shirt that I had worn the day before and zigzagged through the sleeper carriages, arriving at the dining carriage five minutes late. I was the youngest passenger by at least two decades. I sat at the nearest booth to the entrance because all of the other booths were full. The panels above the windows were tinted gold and the words 'Queen Adelaide Restaurant' had been condensed into a jumbled insignia on the glass partition behind my booth.

I stared out the window. Since leaving Perth the previous morning, I'd taken a photograph every hour. I figured the pictures would make a good sixty-fifth birthday present for my dad. So far I'd captured flocks of sheep, water towers, grain silos, dying gum trees and barren pastures. The landscape had changed overnight. All that remained was a seemingly endless terrain of red earth and saltbush.

'Good morning again,' said the young stewardess, placing a laminated menu on the tablecloth. She was wearing a beige collared shirt, a maroon neckerchief and an apron with the restaurant's insignia on it. 'I'm guessing you'd like to start with a coffee,' she said.

'The strongest I'm permitted.'

She didn't laugh as much as I'd hoped.

An elderly man entered the carriage, clutching the upholstery as he shuffled along the aisle. He was wearing a tartan shirt and grey high-waisted trousers. He stopped at the booth where I was seated. 'Do you mind?' he asked.

'Not at all.'

He handed his walking stick to the stewardess and lowered himself to the seat, wincing when his backside touched the cushion. His odour reminded me of musty linen.

'Peter McKaskill,' he said, offering his veiny hand across the table. We shook hands.

The stewardess handed back his walking stick and he placed it across his lap.

'How are you this morning, Pete?' she asked.

'A little under the weather, I'm afraid. But thank you for taking the time to ask.' He let out a chesty cough.

'Can I get you something to eat?'

'Not at this stage,' he said. 'Mind you, I could do with a glass of that cabernet sauvignon from last night.'

The stewardess neglected to write his order on her notepad.

'Never been able to stomach breakfast,' said Pete, fixing his eyes on me drowsily.

I ordered toast with plum jam. The stewardess took my menu and set off towards the kitchen. At the inauguration she had worn a brown, wide-brimmed hat that made her look attainably clumsy, but her gait along the aisle was more assured than any of the passengers.

Pete and I sat silently for several minutes as the cutlery clinked against the table. He had an elongated face with deep-set eyes and heavy bags underneath them. Blood vessels seeped from his sunken cheeks to his nose, merging to form a purple colouration on the ridge. A dark stain permeated his lower lip. There were a number of similar contusions on his forehead.

I looked out the window to avoid his gaze.

'This is the greenest I've seen it,' said Pete.

It didn't look very green.

'Never gets tiring,' he said. 'Mind you, we'd be in a bit of trouble if the train broke down. It'd take a couple of days for them to find us.' He placed an olive-green handkerchief over his mouth and coughed into it.

'My dad used to tell me stories about when he hitched across the Nullarbor back in the seventies,' I said. 'I never really believed how bleak he made it all sound.'

'It's bleak alright,' said Pete, nodding. 'I drove all around the country in a campervan for the best part of ten years and I can promise you, this is as bleak as it gets.' He rubbed his stained lower lip. 'When was the last time you saw a bird out there?'

I looked out the window again. There were four or five mounds of pebbles beside the tracks, but no birds. 'I honestly can't remember,' I said.

'Exactly.' He leant back and exhaled, proud of himself in some strange old man's way. I wasn't sure if it was something about him or just the unusual occurrence of having breakfast with a stranger, but I felt like I had nothing to lose by talking to him. It wasn't a feeling I was used to.

The stewardess returned and placed a cup of coffee in front of me and a glass of red wine in front of Pete. He winked at her.

'Now, if you don't mind me asking,' said Pete, pausing to take a drink, 'what's a handsome young fellow like you doing on this train?'

'I haven't been feeling particularly young lately.'

'Nonsense,' he said, missing my attempted joke. 'You've got your whole life ahead of you.' Looking at the bags under his eyes, it was difficult to refute his point.

'I was lucky enough to come into a bit of money recently,' I said. 'So I guess I'm trying to do something nice for myself and see a bit of the country while I'm at it.'

'And how did you happen to come into a bit of money?' he asked. 'Please stop me if I'm being intrusive.'

'No, it's fine.' I took a sip of coffee. The milk was burnt. 'I won a writing competition,' I said.

'Really? Which one?'

I told him which one.

'That's the one they print in the paper every year, isn't it?'

'It usually gets a run,' I said. 'To be honest, I couldn't quite bring myself to read it in print.'

'I think I might have actually read your story. Was it the one about the miner in Kalgoorlie with the crook back?'

'Yeah, that's the one,' I said, smiling.

Pete took another long drink. 'This is exciting stuff,' he said. 'A real-life writer sitting at my breakfast table.'

I didn't feel like a real-life writer. A photographer from the newspaper had visited me at work shortly before the announcement and lined me up against a steel roller door. He asked me to smile a brooding writer's smile. It occurred to me that I'd have to be an actor, not a writer, to be able to pull that off.

'I thought it was a very skilful piece,' said Pete. 'And I'm not just saying that. You've definitely got a way with words. I remember being very impressed with the first line, even though I've completely forgotten what it was now.'

'*Bluey Randall reckoned he'd seen enough darkness for one lifetime,*' I said.

'That's it. Fantastic opening sentence, tells us everything we need to know about the man.' He coughed into his handkerchief again. 'Looking at you now though, I'm guessing you haven't spent too much time yourself down in the mines. So I'm wondering how it is you got to know all those details.'

'It's mostly just research.'

'Sure,' he said.

I'd spent more time researching degenerative disc diseases in the past six months than I had in pubs, taking the piss out of friends.

'It's just, there were a few small details in there, and maybe I'm reading too much into everything, but there were some things that just felt a bit, I don't know, they just jarred with me. Mind you, it might just have been the mood I was in when I was reading the story.'

'Anything in particular?'

'For starters, there's that part where the main character . . . what's his name again?'

'Bluey,' I said.

'There's the part where Bluey goes to the casino at Burswood on his week off. Now I know it's nice and poetic, him betting all his wages on the roulette table in one hit, but this man, I feel like he knows the value of his money. You show that at the start with him waking up in pain, hoping it'll all be over once he has the surgery.'

Pete cleared his throat. Saliva was gathering at the corners of his mouth. 'What I'm saying is, it all just feels like something that would happen in a story, but maybe not quite in real life. Maybe in real life he doesn't get to have the surgery, but maybe he doesn't end up throwing all his money away at the casino, either. No one throws it all away without a reason.'

He glanced out the window and then looked me in the eye. 'At least, that's the way it seems to me. But I might well be wrong. It wouldn't be the first time.'

He was tapping into one of my greatest fears, namely that the majority of what I wrote would only ever seem like a refined version of the truth. Somehow I wanted it to be more than that.

'Also,' said Pete, not finished yet, 'I understand that you want to show it's all a cycle with this man. He works hard. He plays hard. All that flirty business with the young women is fine, maybe a bit beside the point, but still fine. I suppose what I'm asking is, why should we really care about him, as readers? Why does it mean anything to us when he throws it all away, just for the sake of it?'

'I'm not asking anyone to care about him,' I said, my voice wavering. 'I don't think it's important for a reader to care about a character one way or another.'

'Maybe "care" isn't the right word then. I know characters don't necessarily have to be likeable. Most of us aren't. But surely they've got to make us feel something, or reflect on something, otherwise they're just words and descriptions on a page, taking up our time, and I don't have that much of it left.'

I didn't know how he could be so unaware of the froth that had built up at the corners of his mouth.

'I can see I've upset you,' said Pete. 'Please know it wasn't my intention. Honestly, it's all there in your story. The judges definitely made the right choice. You've set it up for us and it's obvious you know what you're doing. What I'm talking about, or trying to, is the killer punch. If I'm being hypercritical, it just never quite lands that killer punch. That's all.'

I couldn't really think of a greater insult.

'But then again, what do I know?' said Pete, draining the contents of his glass in a way that made my blood boil.

■

Shortly after breakfast, we pulled into a crossing loop to allow a westbound freight through. I tried to pass the time by reading, but I kept repeating the same sentence out loud and I eventually realised it'd be best if I just put the book down. I had always assumed that once my work was in print, I'd be free from self-doubt and that I'd be able to conduct myself with the authority and the silent assurance of someone secretly in the know. What I'd never considered was that the self-doubt might increase.

I was late again after we were summoned to the dining carriage for lunch, so I sat at the same empty booth near the entrance. The menus had already been placed on the table. There was no sign of Pete at any of the other booths. I took another photograph through the window. There were now wider expanses of red earth between the tufts of saltbush.

'It's the writer!' exclaimed Pete, lingering at the carriage door. 'You can't seem to get rid of me, can you?'

He thrust his walking stick at me. His backside made a hollow thud when it hit the cushion. Yellow gunk was pasted to his eyelids.

'Are you sick of it yet?' he asked.

'No.'

'Good attitude.'

The stewardess arrived as I was passing the walking stick back across the table.

'I think you already know what I'm drinking,' said Pete. 'In fact, put a bottle on my account, please.'

The stewardess rolled her eyes at me and smiled. I ordered a glass of water.

'Aren't writers supposed to have a thirst?' asked Pete.

'I guess I'm not a real one then,' I said.

The stewardess took our lunch orders and moved on to the next booth. I tried to see whether she smiled at them in the same way she'd been smiling at me.

'What've you got there?' asked Pete, gesturing at the black case on the table.

'It's just a camera. I've been taking a few photos to show my dad when I get home.'

'What of?'

'Everything, really. I figure it might help to jog a few memories for him. Not that he always needs help.'

Pete stared at the case and exposed the deep furrows on his cheeks. 'About what I said earlier,' he said. 'I get a bit excited sometimes and say things I don't entirely mean. Truth be told, I'm just happy to have someone with young blood sitting opposite me, being forced to listen while I ramble on.'

'It's fine,' I said. 'Forget about it.'

'I will if you will,' he said, probing me with his gunky eyes.

Despite everything, I still had the same feeling that out here in the desert, where not even the birds wanted to brave it, I was free to say anything that crossed my mind without fear of the consequences.

'Ever heard of Cook?' asked Pete.

'No.'

'We'll be stopping there straight after lunch. The town's got a population of four.' He dabbed at the contusions on his temple with a chequered handkerchief. 'Years ago the Kooris used to meet us when we got off the train. They'd sell us boomerangs, rhythm sticks, bullroarers. Anything we liked, really. It was all very civil.'

'How many times have you caught the Indian Pacific, Pete?'

'I've lost count. I try to make it over to Adelaide for Anzac Day every three or four years. This year there's a bit of a reunion of my old squadron. I don't overly enjoy the flight, so I usually have to make do with the train.'

'Does your family live in Perth?'

'There's not really any family in the picture. Not in the way you mean.' He took out the olive-green handkerchief and coughed into it. 'I live in an estate with five other vets out in Joondalup. It's nice and quiet. We all tend to look out for each other. Six gold cards and no wives. If they ever made a show about us, I dare say that's what they'd call it.'

'What's a gold card?'

Pete removed his wallet from his trouser pocket. He folded back the leather tongues and handed me a gold-coloured card. The card had a serial number and the words 'Totally & Permanently Incapacitated' printed on it.

'Thanks,' I said softly, handing it back to him.

'Take a walk up and down the aisle later on,' he said. 'I bet if you asked you'd find half a dozen gold cards on this carriage alone.' He coughed into the handkerchief again.

'Is it enough to get by?'

'It's big,' he said. 'They take good care of us, and so they should.' Pete examined me with his deep-set eyes. His irises seemed somehow more transparent than at breakfast. 'I know what you're thinking. I guess it's good for a writer to be easy to read. You have to understand: the call came, we answered it and, in our own ways, we all paid a price. How can anyone put a sum on that?'

The stewardess returned with my glass of water and Pete's bottle of cabernet sauvignon.

'He's starting to sink his teeth in,' said Pete, shakily pouring himself a glass.

'I find that a bit hard to believe,' she said, turning to me. 'Let me know if he gets too morbid for you.'

'You're already too late,' I said.

I liked the way she laughed. I was starting to feel good about my chances of getting her into a still bed.

'Did you consider not answering the call?' I asked when she was well out of earshot.

'It wasn't really an option. Or it wasn't an option I felt I had any right to take. You're forgetting, most men back then felt the same way.'

'My dad didn't. He ended up in prison.'

'Why wasn't he a conscientious objector?' asked Pete.

'I guess, in the end, he thought that course of action was insufficient. He and some of his friends burnt the letters notifying them of their conscription.'

Pete nodded several times. 'Your father was one of the smart ones.'

'You wouldn't say that if you knew him.'

'No, you have to trust me. We had no idea what we were doing over there. We did some terrible things.'

At school I'd read about a necklace decorated with human tongues.

'I'm man enough to admit it now,' said Pete. 'At first I was just excited to have a tobacco allowance and to listen to the rumble of the old Caribous.' He caught me studying the contusions on his lower lip. 'I should've had an inkling at some point. It was only when they were flying us over the delta of Saigon that I first had the thought: *I've made a terrible mistake. My brain has made a terrible, terrible mistake.* Of course, by then it was too late. A chain of events had already been set in motion.'

Pete drained his glass in one hit and poured another. He tilted the bottle in my direction, but I shook my head. We both stared out the window. I figured we must have crossed the state border by now, which meant it was the first time in my life that I'd been outside Western Australia.

The stewardess eventually arrived with our lunch. As she laid the plates on the tablecloth, she glanced at Pete, but he didn't even acknowledge her. I expected her expression to soften into a smile when she looked my way. It didn't.

Pete took two bites of his toasted sandwich and pushed his plate into the middle of the table. 'You're welcome to finish mine, if you're still hungry.'

'I think I'll be fine,' I said. The thought of sharing his saliva made my own meal hard to stomach.

'Did you work after you came home?' I asked.

'Of course I did,' said Pete. His mouth was still full of puréed bread. 'The last thing I wanted was to have time on my hands. I worked as a service technician in Albany for twelve years. I dipped my toe into the mining sector up in Goldsworthy. I was a field manager for Telstra for the best part of a decade, all across the wheat belt.'

He took another long drink. Abandoned freight carriages were starting to appear along the rail siding.

'One evening I pulled into the garage and I just knew. After thirty-two years of faithful marriage, it was over. I walked into the kitchen and told my wife she could have everything: the house, our friends, the money, the kids. I couldn't do it anymore. I took the campervan we'd bought for when I retired and drove off into the night. I guess the campervan was my one luxury in the end.

'It's a funny thing. As I was driving that night, I accepted that I was alone and that was the end of it. In a way it made me free. There wasn't any animosity towards anyone. Every mistake that ever happened to me was my own doing. I think in time my wife probably accepted it, or understood it somehow. I couldn't really say. There was no point keeping things going on those terms. There never is.'

'Have you seen her since?' I asked.

'I've never really felt the urge. As it happens, she got in contact with me just before last Christmas. I'm not sure how she found me. I knew it had to be serious news, so I let her say her piece. I owed her that much. It turned out my firstborn, Alastair, had gone ahead and hung himself. His wife found him, poor woman. Poor soul.' Pete coughed into his olive-green handkerchief again.

'The thing she seemed the most upset about, my wife, was that Alastair hadn't left a note. I don't know why it made her any sadder than his actual passing. A note wouldn't have changed anything. She said she kept thinking about all the things she could have done differently. To me, that's not a constructive way to think. Mind you, I didn't say that. I didn't really say anything.'

He exhaled and looked me in the eye. 'You might think this is cruel on my part, but when she started crying, I hung up. There wasn't anything else I could do. I knew it ended the minute I left, or maybe even a long time before all of that.'

'I'm sorry, Pete.'

'You don't have to be sorry. I can't even be sure that I'm sorry. I know I'm supposed to be sorry, but to me it's just a word that people have been trained to say. I did what I had to do at the time and, in a way, I already knew the consequences would catch up with me sooner or later.'

There was a rush of static over the intercom. *'We're now arriving in the town of Cook to drop off a mailbag and replenish the train's water supplies,'* announced the driver. *'We'll be stopped for approximately forty-five minutes. When you're walking in the main street of town, please make sure you watch out for the traffic.'*

The Queen Adelaide Restaurant filled with muted laughter.

'He always cracks that joke,' said Pete gloomily.

As the train slowed to a halt, I caught sight of a rusted fridge on the platform. An inscription on the fridge read: OUR HOSPITAL NEEDS YOUR HELP. GET SICK! I quickly got my camera out of its case and pointed it at the fridge.

'Before you stretch your legs,' said Pete, 'why don't you take a picture of your harshest critic?'

I panned the camera around to him and tried to fit his long face into the frame. The shot was horribly out of focus, and I wondered whether it was best that way.

BURNT
HILL
FARM

The sun slides towards the dark mountains like an egg down a hot frying pan, as Don likes to observe to his wife Maggie and their friends Ian and Lesley Sinclair. He can feel the sweat starting to dry on his skin and turn cold. He's been trying to chop as much wood as he can so the new owners will have plenty to get them started. It was nice of Maggie to let him make an offer on the farm, but she knew they'd come up short. It's madness that anyone had to put a price on it all. What's the clean air worth? What's the history of tens of thousands of goldminers worth? What are the kangaroos at dusk worth? Nothing that any six-figure sum can cover, that's for sure.

It's been years since the boys kicked the footy while they watched the sunset. The kids never understood the importance of the ritual. But they will someday. Christ, they've all grown up quickly. Not that anyone doesn't. That's the thing about time. Everyone is always saying how it moves so fast, but maybe fast is just the normal way that it moves. Fast isn't even really fast, if you stop to think about it. The main thing that slows down is the damn tongue. When was it that he started confusing people's names? And why does it make his kids so irritated?

At least the garden bed is finally getting some peace. The problem is that the previous owners planted it smack bang in the middle of the paddock, not knowing it was going to become a footy oval at Easter every year. Apologising for the damage has never been much fun. Still, in the twenty-one years they've been renting the farmhouse, they've never lost any of their bond and they've always been welcome back the next Easter with the garden bed looking immaculate.

And now there is no next Easter. Not at Burnt Hill Farm, anyway. He can't imagine Easter without drifting out to the woodshed late in the afternoon and letting rip. No therapy like it. He tried to show the kids how to do it when they were younger, but they were scared of the spiders. It's probably because they've been over-mothered, which, he can admit from experience, is better than being neglected.

Chopping wood for the fire is something he looks forward to all year round. Easter only really ends once the smell of the fire has disappeared from the clothes he wore at the farm.

Sometimes he avoids washing his jumpers for weeks so he can enjoy the smell just a little longer. But you can cling to things all you like. He sees that now. In the end everything slips away, just like that beautiful sun sliding towards the dark mountains.

IAN, 1989

That first year the adults found themselves staying up long after they'd put the little buggers to bed, sitting in the kitchen with the big pot-bellied stove, drinking tea, berating the Liberal Party, listening to Nina Simone, Joni Mitchell and Bob Dylan on the cassette player that Ian had bought Lesley for their ten-year anniversary. Lesley was becoming even more stunning with age. Ian still couldn't believe his luck. Maggie was a gem, too. Don could be a serious bastard sometimes, but it probably wasn't easy always worrying about whether the bookshop was going to stay afloat.

Ian considered Don and Maggie his best friends. They'd all met at university and attended the Moratorium marches together. There was even a bit of street theatre involved. Now, when their friends were divorcing left, right and centre, the four of them had managed to stick it out. None of them were big drinkers. Maybe that meant something, maybe it didn't. What mattered most, in the end, was trust, and they all had it. There was warmth in that kitchen at night; the kind an unlucky person might go their whole life without knowing.

The mornings were a thing of beauty, too. Nice and nippy. Ian loved the cock-a-doodle-doo of the roosters right outside their window, and the rosellas that hung around the back porch late in the afternoon. Sometimes at dusk he saw kangaroos in the neighbour's paddock, bounding towards the forest. Kangaroos were beautiful movers. Lesson plans and essay-marking barely crossed his mind. Hell, he could even put up with the lingering stench of Don's shit in the toilet all morning.

What Ian loved most, though, was watching the kids play in the mullock mounds behind the farmhouse, where the miners had pillaged the hillside during the gold rush. He could see the possibilities of the terrain through their eyes. The three of them were so at ease with each other. It was as if Kat and William were the siblings Tom never got to have. Ian had always seen himself having four or five kids, a bit of a Brady Bunch, but what did it matter if they'd had to stop at one? People had it a lot worse. That much was clear to him with four days and twenty acres of bliss at his convenience.

KAT, 1990

The Easter Farmhouse was heaps colder than the houses in the city. You could see yourself breathing. They didn't have TV in the country at all. But they had real kangaroos, like Skippy the Bush Kangaroo. It was kind of fun playing with the boys, even though they could be so annoying sometimes. William picked his nose and swallowed it. Every time you picked your nose, you picked away a bit of your brain. Maybe that was why he was so stupid. Tom was scared of Spinney the windmill, but Dad said Spinney's job was to help get water out from the ground, so he was really everyone's friend.

Writing songs about the Easter bunny was so much fun. Every year Kat got to write a new one with Dad so they could sing it to everyone at the barbecue on Sunday. They'd come up with the words together and Kat would make up the dance moves by herself. All the adults clapped at the end and said how clever the song was and how pretty the dancing looked. She was a really good dancer because she did ballet lessons every Thursday after school. She was going to be a ballerina when she was older and maybe an actress and a singer too.

Mum always teased afterwards that Dad's singing hurt her ears, but he wasn't really that bad. He never broke any windows like in the cartoons. He was good at lots of other things, too, like being the boss of a whole bookshop and chopping wood in the shed with the spiders and putting newspaper in the fire so it made everyone warm at dinner. One time he killed a whole family of snakes that were trying to come into the Easter Farmhouse and eat everyone.

Dad was better than Mum because he didn't care when Kat had her Humpty Dumpty egg for breakfast instead of Weet-Bix. Mum said children vomited if they had too much chocolate for breakfast. But she wasn't as scary as Tom's mum. When Kat needed to wee in the middle of the night and she was scared of the mice in the kitchen, she always woke Dad up to carry her to the toilet because otherwise the mice might chew off all her toes, thinking they were peanuts. It had already happened to a friend of hers.

LESLEY, 1991

It was always Maggie who summoned the kids to the back porch by saying, 'You'll never guess who I just saw hopping in the forest.' She put on the kind of fake enthusiastic voice that Lesley imagined her using when she was bathing clients. They hid the eggs together first thing on Sunday morning. Buying Cadbury Mini Eggs from Kmart was as close to consumerism as Ian and Lesley ever permitted themselves to slip. Unlike Don and Maggie, they didn't fall for Father's Day or Mother's Day or any other day that was invented for retail purposes.

Kat, Tom and William would set off with plastic bowls in their hands, scouring the flowerbeds and the pot plants on the bluestones, listening to the silly clues that Ian and Don yelled out. It was nice to see Tom smiling and having fun, but the fact that it was all based on such a fanciful premise frustrated Lesley. She made the kids divide their eggs at the end of the hunt because Tom tended to dominate.

Tom was the first to figure out that there was no bunny. 'How can one animal make it all the way around the world in a night?' he asked Lesley, straight after the hunt. She took him on a walk along the fence line and they eventually settled in the shade of the crabapple trees. She plucked a small apple and shared it with him as she explained the truth about the bunny. Every so often she caught him sneaking a look at the windmill that Ian had nicknamed Spinney, whose rusty metal fangs had literally frightened the shit out of Tom when they first visited the farm.

His lips started quivering when he realised there was no Santa, either. For once, she let him cry. It was strange seeing him drop the bravado that he always maintained around William. Had they made the right decision to let him believe? One of the kids at Lesley's kindergarten said she knew the Easter bunny was coming soon when the Creme Egg ads with the angry teacher started coming on TV. If only kids could be raised to believe in other things with such conviction, the world might have been a better place.

WILLIAM, 1992

Girl germs made you sick and the last thing William wanted was to get sick at the Easter Farmhouse. That's why him and Tom couldn't let Kat play Army with them. Not even as a nurse. They had wars to fight in the forest where the Easter bunny escaped every year. There were whole armies after them. Plus real-life Indians. You had to be brave to fight in wars. If you weren't brave, your country lost automatically and you had to give up your land and your homes and become slaves. It was lucky they never lost.

They were really good at creeping out of the house when the adults were making dinner. There was a trench behind the garden bed where they could hide from all their enemies. If you put black crayon under your eyes, it was impossible for anyone else to see you in the dark. But they could still see each other. They had chocolate-chip muesli bars that were flown in for them on green helicopters. You could make grenades out of mud. Tom always got to throw the first one because he was older and he had a higher ranking. Then they had to get down really low and block their ears with their fingers.

They were changing history by beating the mean Turkish people at Gallipoli. Tom said the whole country would be proud of them. Once they got home, they were going to get covered in medals and people would cheer for them in the streets when they were old men. The more enemies you killed, the more medals you got to wear. It made William so happy and excited that he pissed his pants with laughter.

The adults forced them to stay out in the rain on Easter Sunday, cleaning the mud grenades off the house. Mum and Dad were so much meaner when they were around Tom's parents. They didn't even let them do the hunt, so Kat got all the mini eggs to herself and she didn't have to share. He was going to write a letter to the Easter bunny about it, saying how him and Tom were only protecting their country. If you protected your country, you were automatically a hero.

TOM, 1993

It was good that William still believed in the Easter bunny because it meant they got to have the hunt. Having to share was a crappy idea. What you found should be what you got. It wasn't Tom's fault that he always found the most eggs. Dad said the goldminers always got to keep what they found, so why didn't he? There was still lots of gold left around the farmhouse that the miners had missed, and Tom and William were digging holes so they could find it. Then their parents could all move into mansions and say thank you to them.

Kicking the footy with William was good, too, even though Tom could kick it way further. Next year he was going to play under-elevens for a real team. They gave everyone medals at the end of the season. He already had two medals from Little Athletics. Kat didn't play any sport because ballet wasn't really a sport. She was fat and annoying and her dancing at the barbecue was crap, even if Mum and Dad wouldn't let him say so in front of anyone. Girls weren't very good at anything. He hoped he'd never have to have a girlfriend.

If he did have to have a girlfriend, it would probably be William's mum. He accidentally saw some parts of her that he wasn't supposed to see. They were different to his mum's parts. He thought no one was in the toilet, but when he opened the door to poo, she was in there with her undies around her feet. She covered the part where you wee from, but she wasn't really that mad because she smiled. Mum didn't think it was funny. She said he had to remember to knock first and made him say sorry to William's mum.

William's dad was always chopping wood in the woodshed so they could have a fire at night. The sound was really loud and it echoed and the wood always split in half straight down the middle. Chopping wood made William's dad more of a man than Tom's dad. William's dad would probably win if they had a fight because he was bigger and he was more used to being in an angry mood.

MAGGIE, 1994

Kat and William started screaming just after they'd commenced their annual inspection of the farmhouse. Maggie found them in the living room, watching Coyote chase Road Runner in vain all across the American desert. Kat asked why Channel Nine was called Win in the country. The owners hadn't mentioned the telly, so there wasn't any time for Maggie and Don to present a unified front. They decided to let it slide for the time being, at least while they unpacked, so they could finally get some peace from the kids.

By the time Ian and Lesley arrived, the telly had already been on for hours. Even though they initially didn't say anything, which was always their way, Maggie could tell they weren't happy about it. After the kids went to bed, they had a long debate in the kitchen about the new appliance. Lesley was in favour of banning it. Ian suggested there should be no television during the day. Maggie was inclined to let the kids make their own choices, but she would have been just as happy to put an axe through the damn thing.

Don focused on keeping the fire going, stoking it just for the sake of it half the time. Maggie knew he was thinking what a shame it was that they weren't spending the first night catching up on each other's lives. It was true. But if there was one thing she'd learnt from being a disability support worker, it was that people had to deal with the complications that life threw at them. Don had always had a lot of trouble accepting the complications in his life. She already knew it would end with him exploding at her, like he exploded whenever the Macintosh computer froze on him, as though life itself was out to get him and him alone.

In the end they opted for Ian's suggestion. Lesley draped a towel over the telly first thing every morning, which might have been a good tactic at the kindergarten. On the last night they all crowded into the living room to watch a movie. It was about a slobbery dog that moved in with a boring suburban family. The kids loved it. Maggie could sense Ian and Lesley's silent judgement in the air. She hated being made to feel like a bad person. There were plenty worse than her out there. At least her kids had enough awareness to knock before storming into the bathroom.

DON, 1995

Then there was the year that the ABC was shooting a miniseries based on Banjo Paterson's 'The Man from Snowy River' in the local ranges. Several cast members, including one famous Australian actor, had been staying at Burnt Hill Farm during the shoot. But they all had to book accommodation elsewhere over Easter so that Don, Maggie, Ian, Lesley, Tom, Kat and William could take up their annual booking. Don kept joking, 'Not even the man from Snowy River can get rid of us.'

His joy was short-lived, though. On Saturday morning Tom woke up complaining about a pain in his stomach. He wasn't hungry at lunch and William said, 'I think Tom's really sick, Dad.' William didn't even try to talk Tom into kicking the footy with him. By late afternoon Tom looked so pale that Ian and Lesley rushed him back to a hospital in the city. His appendix was taken out on the morning of Easter Sunday.

The farm felt empty without Ian, Lesley and Tom, especially at sunset. Maggie did her line about the Easter bunny, even though no one believed in it anymore. Kat and William refused to divide their eggs after the hunt and spent most of the time bickering about whose turn it was to choose the television channel. When had Kat become so invested in the lives of the characters on *Home and Away* and *Neighbours*? No one even mentioned writing an Easter song.

Don tried to teach William how to chop wood, but he spent the whole time peppering Don with questions about how someone could stay alive without an appendix. He was a bit of a funny kid. It was a relief that his army phase had run its course, but turning his fixations to Tom's appendix didn't necessarily seem like a step towards normality. At least he was only nine years old. They'd probably all laugh about it at his twenty-first birthday party. Maybe Tom would even make a joke about it in his speech.

There was something strange about the way Maggie walked to the dam in the afternoon to read her book. Was she bored with him? Don marvelled at the fact that this woman who slept soundlessly beside him at night, with ankles that were bigger than he'd have liked, had once induced a ravenous desire in him, to the point where he felt that all life would have stopped if it had remained unrequited. He knew it was the kind of sentiment that could never be voiced. An empty space was slowly opening up inside his chest. They might as well have let the famous actor stay at the farmhouse.

LESLEY, 1996

Then there was the year that Lesley's old grape-picking friends, Drew and Gillian, accepted her invitation to the Sunday barbecue. They'd all met in the Barossa Valley when Lesley was nineteen. She was more carefree back then. Drew and Gillian arrived at the farmhouse in a dusty Range Rover. They'd driven down from Kununurra, where they managed an Aboriginal art gallery, camping along the way to fish for cod. The first thing Lesley noticed was that Drew's shoulder-length hair had started to go grey.

An old kelpie hopped out of the back of the Range Rover. His collar had a tag that read: ATTICUS. Lesley had never been a good judge of a dog's character. She didn't know whether to be more worried by the damage Atticus might do to the flowerbeds or the threat he posed to the kids. But as the afternoon wore on, all Atticus really seemed interested in was resting at Drew's feet and accepting the little chunks of sausage that Ian thought he was offering on the sly.

Don, Maggie and Ian had lots of questions for the glamorous new bush couple. Do the locals accept you? How do you find buyers for the Aboriginal paintings? Isn't it a bit remote up north? Drew and Gillian seemed amused that their lives should be considered in any way out of the ordinary. It was strange for Lesley seeing her two old friends look so at ease around each other. She assumed living in the bush had done it to them. They were probably the least pretentious people she'd ever met.

The kids occasionally surfaced to smother a sausage in sauce or scull a glass of soft drink. Kat and William liked patting Atticus. They'd been nagging Maggie to buy them a puppy for years. Lesley was surprised Maggie hadn't given in. Tom kept staring at Gillian, whose red hair splashed around in the haze of autumn sunlight. It made sense that Drew loved her. There was dirt beneath his fingernails. He didn't seem to mind eating with Atticus's saliva all over his hands.

Lesley had once kissed Drew by a barrel fire at night. They were both pissed. He tasted like red wine and tobacco. At the time she thought that she was too bland to try to take things further. It was a little disconcerting watching the Range Rover recede through a cloud of dust that afternoon. Looking after twenty-five germy kids for a living suddenly didn't feel all that important. She couldn't help but imagine that this life of dirt roads, pitching tents, squatting in bushes, mosquito bites, fishing and wet bodies might have belonged to her if she'd been just a little more courageous.

WILLIAM, 1997

Then there was the year that Tom wanted to include Kat in everything they did. It was probably because his mum and dad had said something to him. They were always telling him how he was meant to act. He wasn't even allowed to watch *Blue Heelers*. Kat was really mean. She got in big trouble with Dad when she got her tongue pierced and she never ate food anymore because she thought she was fat. Plus she smoked cigarettes when she was babysitting and she said she was going to get addicted to heroin when she was older.

Everyone was being so boring. Sometimes Tom said he didn't want to kick the footy, even though he really did want to. He was different since he got his appendix out. His scar had got better, but it was still going to be there forever. He was lucky his appendix didn't explode inside him. It could happen. The adults were being more boring than Tom. They always talked about politics in the kitchen and their music was so stupid. On one of their CDs the man couldn't even sing properly.

William invented a new game by counting how many kicks it took him to kick the footy from the front gate to the clothesline. The last kick had to go in the middle of the trees where the cord hung from, otherwise it didn't count. It was heaps of fun. He could play all day and he forgot how annoying everyone was being. The least kicks he did from the front gate to the clothesline was seven, but three of them were perfect torpedos and usually he couldn't do it in less than nine.

On the last morning, while the adults were packing the cars, he accidentally kicked the footy into Ian and Lesley's bedroom window and broke it. He'd thought it was a good angle to try a banana kick from, but it came off his shoe wrong. He ran and hid in the grass near the dam where all the snakes slept at night. Was he too old to be smacked? It was hard to think of an excuse that would stop Dad from swearing like he always did at Kat.

MAGGIE, 1998

Then there was the year that Maggie and Lesley started going for long walks in the afternoon. Lesley suggested it. She said walking helped to keep her knee from stiffening up. Maggie couldn't remember how many years it had been since they'd spent any one-on-one time together. Every day they'd set off at four o'clock and walk in a new direction. They walked to the crabapple trees, through the forest and around the dam where Lesley had found William the year before, curled up in a ball with tears in his eyes.

They exchanged stories about the magazines they'd found in their children's bedrooms. Lesley mocked Tom for his obsession with big-breasted women. Maggie suspected William wasn't interested in breasts. But at least she no longer feared he'd be responsible for the next Port Arthur-style massacre. She confessed that some days she felt like reaching into Kat's mouth and ripping her tongue ring out. It was nice to laugh together. They never really talked about their husbands, even though she knew that's what Ian and Don thought the whole thing was about.

On the final afternoon, they decided to walk in the middle of the gravel road. Sunlight squeezed through the tall branches. It was already starting to get a bit chilly. Although they walked mostly in silence, Maggie got the impression that Lesley didn't want to turn back either. She wanted to propose that they start going on regular bushwalks when they got home. Maybe once a month. But she didn't want to exhaust Lesley's goodwill.

They eventually wandered into the forest and stopped by the remains of a burnt-out cottage. All that was left standing was the chimney. Lesley sat on the ground and sighed. There were so many lines on her forehead. It was difficult to think of her as being in her mid-forties. 'Why do you think it is that we all stay together?' she asked, shuffling dry gum leaves around with her feet. 'You know, you and Don and me and Ian. What makes us last?' Even though Maggie would have liked to say something profound, she couldn't really think of a good explanation. 'Maybe we're just committed people,' she said.

Lesley told her about kissing Drew by the barrel fire all those years ago and how sometimes she caught herself wondering what might have been. 'That's nothing,' said Maggie, smiling. 'He can leave his shoes under my bed any time.' They both laughed. She felt certain that Lesley understood her better than anyone else in the world. They were actually pretty similar. In the end they had to hurry back so they wouldn't miss the sunset.

TOM, 1999

Then there was the year that Kat brought her friend Felicity to the farm. Both girls had dyed black hair and they were both obsessed with a Nick Cave album that only had songs about killing people. Tom didn't see how any of the songs were catchy. Still, he liked the way the two girls were always teasing him about stuff he didn't know. The three of them hung out in the mounds behind the farmhouse at night, where he and William used to play Army and dig for gold. Tom had no idea how much the adults knew about what they were up to, but

Kat and Felicity didn't seem to give a shit if their clothes smelt of cigarettes.

The girls had smuggled a jar of magic mushrooms and two bottles of Jim Beam in their backpacks. They decided to take the mushrooms the night before Easter Sunday. Tom wasn't in the right mood to have any, but he was happy to sit out the back and drink bourbon with them. William gave Tom a sad look when Tom invited him, like everything was moving way too fast for him. But no one could kick a footy forever.

Felicity said the sky was spinning out of control and she was seeing lots of other things that weren't really there. Then she started vomiting. Kat was a pro at taking drugs. She talked to Tom about how her family didn't really understand her and lots of other stuff that no one had ever talked to him about. It made him feel funny. She even wanted to see the scar on his stomach. She ran her fingers over it and then kept running them down into his boxers. Then she kissed him with her tongue and made sounds like she was enjoying it.

Her breath smelt like cans of really sweet Coke. She knew exactly what she was doing. She told him not to be nervous and showed him where to put his hands. He clung to her hips and watched her head bob up and down in front of the blurry stars. Did women always keep their eyes closed during it? He tried to last as long as he could. This, he felt certain, was love.

KAT, 2000

Then there was the year that Kat asked Maggie to give her driving lessons. There was nothing else to do on the farm now that she wasn't allowed to bring friends anymore. She was happy to avoid Tom. He was always staring at her with his pathetic puppy-dog eyes. William was always doing his homework. He was such a fucking nerd. She didn't want Don to teach her how to drive because he'd just lose his temper. He was so loud when he was angry and other times he looked so quiet and depressed. But he tried to hide it from Ian and Lesley on the farm because he must have known that if they saw him like that, they wouldn't want to be his friends.

Every morning she and Maggie spent half an hour sputtering along the driveway in the white Corolla. They'd finish by practising reversing and parallel parking near the woodshed where Don got out some of his anger in the afternoon. Maggie was so patient. She still called Kat 'sweetie' when she was giving her instructions. It was nice that she never got angry about the piercings. Kat could tell, without a word being said, that her mum was shit-scared she was going to get a tattoo once she turned eighteen.

On the final morning, as Maggie was explaining why it was so important to slow down on dirt roads, Kat realised how pretty her mum was in a natural kind of way. She must have had the chance to fuck a lot of guys when she was younger, particularly with the whole free love thing in the sixties and seventies. Why did she even stay with Don? He was always pissing and moaning about the bookshop and he looked so weird when he watched the sunset. It was actually embarrassing thinking about how they used to sing Easter songs together.

'We'll buy you a car once you get your licence,' said Maggie. 'No, don't,' said Kat. 'You've already done enough.' She was more interested in finding a way to get to Europe. She'd been saving up by stacking shelves at Coles. It was okay work as long as she was stoned. She could see herself flying over to Europe and never coming back. She'd miss Maggie, but there was no one else she'd miss in this small, backward, bogan country where people couldn't even be who they really were.

IAN, 2001

Then there was the year that Tom brought his new girlfriend, Grace, to the farm. She was a private-school girl, which didn't sit too well with Lesley. God knew why she was interested in Tom. She didn't like that they all had to share the same toilet, and she got disproportionately flustered when they ran out of hot water on the second morning. But the worst thing of all, as far as Ian was concerned, was that she'd never heard Paul Kelly's music.

Tom and Grace retreated to the living room straight after dinner every night. They didn't even want to stay up for some Tim Tams and a chat. Ian insisted that they sleep on separate mattresses and he had already warned Tom that there wasn't to be any funny business. He hadn't done any funny business of his own until he met Lesley. He knew he was on to a good thing because of how nurturing she was at the beginning. Not that anyone at the farm would have guessed it from the way she spoke about George W. Bush at dinner.

Ian felt sorry for William, who spent most of his time cooped up in the bedroom with the horrible pink wallpaper. What sort of sixteen-year-old knew they wanted to study medicine? He couldn't pinpoint the exact year when Tom and William had stopped kicking the footy. He sensed the boys apathy to one another was a sticking point for Don and Maggie, too. There was also a strange tension between Grace and Kat, even though they were polite enough to each other most of the time. At the barbecue on Sunday, they had a heated debate about the merits of body art, which only ended when Kat stormed off and hurled her sausage against the side of the farmhouse.

On the final night, Lesley flat out admitted that she didn't like Grace. She was adamant that it wasn't going to last. As Lesley spoke softly, knowing how thin the walls were, Ian wondered if she was projecting some of her own discontentment on to the poor girl. He knew he'd never know. Even though Tom dated

Grace for the next four years, and they were briefly engaged, she never came back to Burnt Hill Farm.

DON, 2002

Then there was the year that Kat asked Don to walk to the dam with her. When had she started calling him Don, not Dad? She'd spent her teenage years angry with him for reasons that escaped him. The more he tried to understand, the angrier it seemed to make her. She was about to fly to London, and any warmth that the request ought to have sparked in him was counteracted by his fear that some home truth was about to be delivered.

They walked in silence through the rye grass, careful to watch out for snakes, then settled on the dry clay by the dam. The water level was much lower than Don had expected. It was a very peaceful spot. He could see why Maggie had liked to read there all those years ago and how it mightn't have been as much of an affront to him as he'd thought at the time.

Once they got talking, they talked for over an hour. It was just like when Kat wanted to be a dancer, a singer and an actress. She even teased him for not having a mobile phone; not that he could see what he'd use it for. Don was too afraid to press for a reason why he was being afforded such a pleasant allotment of daughterly time. Then finally, while he was explaining why he didn't need an electronic database at the bookshop, Kat said, 'You know I had an abortion, right?'

Of all the questions that flashed through his wounded mind, all he could think to ask was, 'When?' She told him it was when she was sixteen. He didn't know how he'd missed it, but he knew it was his fault in some way and he knew he'd never forgive himself. He used to feed this girl the froth from his cappuccino with a teaspoon and he used to start writing lyrics for their Easter songs a month before Easter. How could it have all gone so wrong?

When he didn't say anything else, Kat started skipping yonnies across the water. She wasn't even close to crying. There had been life in her tummy beneath that God-awful bellybutton ring. It was the most harrowing thought of his life. 'Does your mum know?' he asked at last. 'She drove me there,' said Kat.

TOM, 2003

Then there was the year that Lesley brought her friend Marcia from the kindergarten along. Marcia's husband of twelve years had recently left her for his legal secretary. Her wrists looked too skinny to Tom. Even though it put a dampener on the whole holiday, he understood why his parents had invited her. They were good people. Some of the people he was starting to make friends with at uni reminded him of them, always talking about forcing the prime minister to say sorry and how greenhouse gases were going to ruin the planet.

Marcia spent Sunday morning singing in the kitchen, preparing a pear and walnut salad for the barbecue. At lunch Tom overheard her telling Lesley that she should have seen the signs. Marcia spent the rest of the afternoon in the living room. No one touched the walnut salad, but Maggie emptied a third of it into the rubbish bin to be polite. He could still remember what Maggie looked like sitting half-naked on the toilet, trying to cover herself up. In a strange way, he found the memory more enticing than any he had of Grace.

Out of boredom, Tom asked Don if he could teach him how to chop wood. Don kept crapping on about how important it was to let your top hand slide down the axe. He said the actors could never get it right in the movies. Tom knew he looked flimsy with the axe in his hands, and he was terrified that he was going to drive the thing into his shins. He slowly learnt to trust himself. The funny thing was, he'd always assumed that whatever logs Don chopped went straight into the fire that night. But Don said it was important to let the wood dry out, and they probably never even got to use any of the logs he chopped.

The next morning Tom caught Marcia lingering near the woodshed, watching him clumsily wield the axe. He decided not to mention it to his parents. But he couldn't sleep that night. He kept imagining another meeting at the woodshed with Marcia, getting to know her skeletal form against the stumps of wood. Somehow he didn't think she'd be afraid of the spiders.

Tom eventually got out of bed and made his way cautiously along the pitch-black hallway. He thought he could hear mice in the kitchen. He lingered outside the door to the living room, picturing Marcia's bony ribs going up and down as she slept. He bet she knew things he'd never even dreamt of. How could anyone cheat on her? There were so many things in life just like this, waiting right there for him to take, if only he wanted them badly enough.

LESLEY, 2004

Then there was the year of the big HECS argument. Lesley, Ian, Don and Maggie stayed up late the first night, catching up on their lives and firing each other up about the senselessness of the Iraq War. It made Lesley worry about the planet they were leaving to their children and their children's children. They'd all attended the big demonstrations in the city, even though they were never going to sway Bush and Blair and all those other puppets who thought a war on terror was anything other than an oxymoron.

It got Ian reminiscing about all the protests they'd attended in their uni days and how an education used to be a free and eye-opening experience. He worried that, given Tom was doing a bloody arts degree, he was going to spend the rest of his life with a HECS debt hanging over his head. Lesley knew there was something strange in the silence from across the table. 'Aren't you worried about Kat and William?' she asked. Not that Kat was interested in anything other than travelling, getting pissed and asking for handouts.

'We paid up front for William,' said Maggie, avoiding making eye contact. It didn't have to be something to be ashamed of, which made Maggie's reaction even more frustrating. Lesley knew that Maggie was propping up the bookshop with the money from her parents' estate, but she hadn't realised how flush they were. If they were so well off, why didn't they get solar panels put on their roof? She could feel her limbs starting to shake. Her knee was killing her. No wonder Tom and William had drifted apart. They probably both knew they were destined for different worlds.

'No, seriously, that's great,' said Lesley. 'But don't ever make any excuses for him.' Ian gave her thigh a quick squeeze under the table. Maggie looked like she was about to start crying, which wasn't going to solve anything. Lesley felt certain that it'd be the last time they all visited the farm. And bloody Don just sat there turning logs over in the fire, feeling sorry for himself as usual, as though there weren't much bigger issues in the world that deserved his attention.

WILLIAM, 2005

Then there was the year that Don pleaded with William to change his mind about not coming to the farm. In the end William gave in, not that he condoned the emotional wreck that his dad had become. He didn't understand why Don had to read the obituaries in the paper every morning, like he wanted grief to arrive on his doorstep. There was plenty of time for grief. William had already seen his share at the clinical school. The amputee ward was the hardest to stomach. Sometimes living didn't seem like the most humane option.

It took him a few days to relearn how to relax. Dad always accused him of seeming preoccupied, but he didn't see what William was up against at uni. Preoccupied was the least he had to be. Mum made him a strawberry smoothie after breakfast every morning. It was nice to be mothered again. He could tell she was proud of him. He hadn't given them half the trouble that Kat had over the years. Did they even know the whole truth about her?

Ian forced Lesley to talk to William about a pain in her knee that had been keeping her up at night. William tried to examine her in the same composed, scrupulous manner as the doctors he'd been observing at the clinic. As he was bending and straightening Lesley's leg in the kitchen, testing its function, he expected Ian to start making wisecracks about foot massages.

But he didn't. It was strange how all of a sudden everyone had stopped treating him like a child just because of what he was studying to become.

He finally managed to succumb to the mood of the farm late on Sunday afternoon, lying on the grass under the clothesline, sharing a six-pack of Coopers with Tom. Tom had been at it all day. He gave William shit about the footy game he used to play by himself around the clothesline, but at least he hadn't been afraid of a windmill. It was funny how neither of them cared about footy anymore.

William admitted that he'd pissed his pants while throwing mud grenades all those years ago. Tom admitted he was having second thoughts about marrying Grace. 'Some days I even start hoping she has an accident on her way home from work,' he said. William knew his old friend wasn't being serious, but if Tom knew what it really meant to be in an accident, and there was one in particular that stuck in his mind, he wouldn't even joke about it.

KAT, 2006

Then there was the year that Kat showed up at the farm with her friend Neela. They'd met working in an Australian pub in London and had been inseparable ever since. It was even harder for Neela; there was no way she could tell her parents back in

Delhi. Kat sure as hell wasn't asking her to. She hadn't even told any of her friends. The only reason William knew was because he'd busted her and a random girl she'd met going at it in the laneway at her farewell drinks.

Don's first question when he was introduced to Neela outside the woodshed was, 'Do you follow the cricket?' Kat apologised to her afterwards. Maggie's eyes went straight to the Hindu tattoo on Neela's neck. They slept in the living room, just like Tom and his stuck-up girlfriend had. Neither of them felt like having sex because Kat's parents were in the next room, but they enjoyed the novelty of sleeping on the floor and having the LCD television on in the background while they chatted late at night.

Kat showed Neela around the farm and explained everything that had happened over the years. She even showed her the spot where she had made the worst mistake of her life, with Tom. It wasn't fun talking about it, but she wanted total disclosure in their relationship so that they wouldn't end up like her parents. As Neela listened to the story, her bold black eyeliner started trickling down her cheeks. When it was over, she put her arm around Kat and stroked her hair, which for the first time in years was its natural colour.

Funnily enough, the first person to say anything about it to Kat was Ian. As she was drying dishes in the kitchen, watching a crimson rosella drink out of the birdbath, he tapped her on the shoulder and said, 'I just want you to know I think it's lovely.'

Even though he sounded ridiculous, she gave him a hug and thanked him.

Kat and Neela held hands at the barbecue on Sunday. Kat tried not to look nervous and tried to be as opinionated as ever when everyone was discussing the Cronulla riots. But she could feel everyone's eyes on them and she was terrified of what Don might think but never have the nerve to say.

MAGGIE, 2007

Then there was the year Ian decided he would write the great Australian novel. By Easter he was already halfway through his annual leave, but he was only up to the fifth chapter. Lesley was being very supportive. She was more reasonable now that she was taking anti-inflammatories. Every morning Maggie entered the kitchen to find Ian hunched over his school-issued laptop, nursing a mug of instant coffee. She'd never seen him with stubble before. His morning smell was even more pungent than Don's, if that was possible.

Maggie and Don made sure they encouraged Ian. But at night Don complained that the whole exercise was self-indulgent and it was rude of Ian to have brought his laptop to the farmhouse. Life as he knew it was a series of small sacrifices, one after another, that had to be made. Seeing Ian working so feverishly on their holiday, writing God knows what, he felt like his friend was spitting in the face of all the sacrifices he had made; sacrifices that denied him such a luxury. Besides, he didn't see how Ian could possibly hope to crack the market at his age.

Maggie didn't bother to argue with Don, because she thought it was all a response, in one way or another, to the Kat situation. So much went unsaid these days. What did it matter whether man loved woman or man loved man or woman loved woman? It was all the same. He couldn't ignore Kat forever just because she wasn't going to give him grandkids. Surely in the end Kat's happiness was more important than his.

Ian explained the plot of his novel to Maggie while they were sitting out on the back porch, drinking tea, during one of his three hour-long breaks for the day. Don was having an afternoon nap. Even though the plot sounded a little convoluted, Ian really believed in the story he had to tell. Maggie glanced at the pot plants and the flowerbeds where she and Lesley used to hide the mini eggs when the kids were little. When was it that they had stopped going on their afternoon walks?

She offered to proofread the opening chapters for Ian. At dinner he presented her with a stack of recycled paper that was already covered in Lesley's handwriting. Tom rolled his eyes. As she slowly read the manuscript in bed that night, she could feel the scorn in Don's silence. Despite Ian's assurances that the story was fictional, all she could imagine in the struggles of the central characters were the lives of Ian, Lesley and Tom.

IAN, 2008

Then there was the year that they suddenly had a full house. Tom brought along his new girlfriend, Stephanie. He never seemed to have any trouble finding them. Keeping them was another thing. But maybe that was just the way of the younger generation. Stephanie was more sociable than the last few and she laughed at all of Ian's jokes. She reminded him a bit of Lesley when she was at university. It wasn't so much the way she looked as the way she threw her head back when she laughed.

Kat and Neela had flown back from Delhi the week before and were about to move into an apartment together. Don and Maggie were even going to put up the bond.

Late on Saturday night, William showed up with a nurse he'd met on his regional placement. She had beautiful blue eyes and it was obvious she loved him from the way she teased him about his awful fashion sense. Things got so crowded that they had to make a bathroom roster for the last two mornings.

Ian loved having everyone under the one roof. If he listened carefully during the day, he could hear sounds coming from every part of the farmhouse. Taps screeching on and off, water rushing along the pipes, windows rattling, old boards squeaking, low voices and that unmistakable rustling in the ceiling. The only problem was that it distracted him from the novel that had eaten its way into his professional life and, fifty-six thousand words in, showed no sign of nearing completion.

Instead of a barbecue on the Sunday, Neela cooked a chicken curry for lunch. She promised to go easy on the chilli powder. Even Don got through his bowl without grimacing. Neela explained to everyone what Diwali was. Maggie asked a lot of questions. Afterwards it started to rain, forcing them all inside for coffee and Tim Tams. As they crowded around the kitchen table, with Ian trying desperately to avoid farting, Tom said he had an announcement to make. He clasped Stephanie's hand and, looking mostly at Lesley, announced that they were expecting their first child.

The ten of them, eleven counting the unborn gem, stayed in the kitchen for hours as the rain bucketed over the garden bed. Don got the fire going and asked if he could feel whether Ian and Lesley's grandkid was kicking. He was a strange bugger sometimes. Stephanie didn't seem to mind. As Ian watched Don pat her knitted sweater, whispering rubbish about literature, sport and politics, he wondered whether he should include the scene somewhere in his novel.

DON, 2009

The sun slides towards the dark mountains like an egg down a hot frying pan. Tom is bouncing little Scarlett up and down on his thighs, talking in that funny language that he and Stephanie think they've invented. What did Maggie used to call the urge to talk nonsense to a baby? She definitely had a name for it. Tom has bags under his eyes now, but maybe those bags are giving his life some purpose at last. Don's priorities changed the second Kat was born. Everything since then has been for her and William, even if they don't see it.

Kat is tickling the bub on the cheek and making faces. She could still be such an amazing mother. But he knows he's got to stop thinking like that. Besides, it's not like she's doing it just to give him the shits. Not like all those bad haircuts and ugly piercings. And at least she doesn't rub his face in it like some of the touchy-feely couples that come into the bookshop.

When is William going to start having kids? He's less serious now that he's in a serious relationship. How on earth did he convince such a beautiful woman to shack up with him? It's hard to imagine him pursuing anyone if it was more practical to be studying. But, at the end of the day, practical is what you want standing by your bedside. It's still incredible to think that people's lives are going to be in his son's hands.

Ian and Lesley are marvelling at every sound that comes out of Scarlett's mouth. It's impossible to talk to them for a whole minute these days without seeing their eyes searching for the bub. They're talking about taking swing-dancing classes once Lesley's back on her feet. It's easy to picture them shuffling around in a room full of twenty-year-olds, out of time with the music, enjoying every second of it.

Is Maggie annoyed that he's never danced with her? It's probably the least of her annoyances. He never meant to give her so many. Sometimes he can hear himself starting up on a rant and at the same time another part of him knows it's not worth going through with it. But there's nothing he can do about it all now. What matters is that they've stood the test of time. They've even stayed together long enough to see a black president of the United States of America.

'Do you mind if I hold Scarlett?' he asks Tom. She groans when he starts cradling her and looks like she's about to start bawling. The pinkie finger should fix it. It always used to calm Kat down. He loves the slippery feel of the bub's saliva. An entire human hand wrapped around his puffy, wrinkled finger. Who would have thought it? The whole thing probably comforts him more than the child.

Everyone goes silent as the golden glow spreads across the paddocks one last time. There's nothing but beauty as far as the eye can see. Even Scarlett senses it. Don tries his best not to cry. He knows that there is still gold in the hills all around the farmhouse and that there always will be.

By Ian Sinclair

JUBILEE
MILE

It was a bit of an impossible situation. At least, that's what Emily's mum called it when she was explaining why Emily would have to catch the bus to school for the first time in four and a half years. If it wasn't for the school play opening the following night—and Emily playing the lead female in it—she was sure her mum would have let her stay home with Aunt Marilyn. She always used to look up to her aunt, who had shown up at their house the night before, unannounced, sporting a black eye.

The bus huffed and puffed its way past Home Timber and Hardware, the Gateway Motor Inn and the rundown timber cottages along the creek. They were stuck behind a truck full of sandbags. It was a freezing morning. The power lines stretched across the grasslands, disappearing into the mist. The parallel pylons looked freaky up close, like something plucked from the pages of an old science-fiction book. Emily had no idea where they started and where they might end.

A group of girls at the back of the bus were making an awful racket, trying to coordinate the harmonies of a song called 'Firework'. Emily had seen the clip on *The Loop* at Maddie's house and it was the most laughable thing ever. One of the girls couldn't hit a high note to save her life. Their wailing was drowning out the song on the driver's radio, which he'd set to a station that played 'classics' from over twenty years ago. Her dad was always listening to the same station when he picked her up from school in the afternoon. Even his singing was better than the girls'.

The bus driver grunted whenever a kid greeted him. Some of the boys from the junior campus sniggered as they walked along the aisle after validating their tickets. It was hard to tell whether the driver gave a crap. He had a greying beard that matched his wiry hair and he kept drinking from a big plastic coffee cup. All of his weight converged at his stomach to form a rounded swell beneath his fluffy red vest. His posture was the worst Emily had ever seen. His cheeks were an inflamed red, almost purple, not unlike her aunt's cheeks.

She watched him stare lifelessly out the windscreen as the bus started climbing the hill, passing the last of the service stations and making its way towards Valley Steel Sales. She spotted Sam Kowalski's house. The after-party was going to be there once they'd bumped out on Friday night. There was a picket sign next to the driveway that read: FIREWOOD RED GUM $150 FREE BAG OF KINDLING. The sign had gone up three months after Sam's mother passed away from breast cancer. Emily felt relieved when he wasn't standing with Maddie at the next stop.

'Oh my God, what are you doing on here?' said Maddie, smothering Emily in a big hug, something she'd only started doing since the summer holidays.

'Mum had some other stuff to do this morning.' She didn't want to mention Marilyn. She hated it when the other kids at school, particularly some of the girls in her year, made a melodrama out of their problems. Most of the time they weren't even real problems.

'I am totally freaking out about the play,' said Maddie.

'You're barely even in it.'

'I know. I'm just worried I'm going to trip over on stage or do something embarrassing in front of everyone.'

Emily laughed and shook her head. 'You'll be fine, trust me.'

'It's easy for you, you're a natural at it.'

'No I'm not,' said Emily. She could feel the colour rising to her cheeks and she hated herself for it.

'Do you mind if we quickly practise our scene?'

Emily shrugged. 'Sure, if you want.'

They ran through their lines twice. Maddie kept stuffing hers up. The bus pulled into the terminus that overlooked the football oval. Emily made a point of thanking the driver before getting off the bus. He didn't respond. Maddie started rehearsing the scene again and Emily listened absently as she breathed in the smell of the eucalypts. She loved the smell of wet bark. It was much nicer than any perfume. She noticed the hideous mural on the wall of the underpass that she'd helped to paint in her first year at the senior campus. Predictably, she'd painted a brown filly galloping towards the winning post.

In English class, her teacher was listing persuasive writing techniques on the whiteboard: inclusive language, alliteration, repetition, use of humour, metaphor and, of course, rhetorical questions. They were all so obvious, thought Emily, her eyes drifting to the window. Three crows were squabbling over a sandwich in the courtyard and an aeroplane glided below the clouds until it disappeared from her line of sight. She was still annoyed about being cast as Oriel Lamb. Why hadn't they let her play Dolly Pickles? There hadn't even been any auditions. Once, just once, she wanted to play a train wreck, cheating on her husband, fighting with her daughter, staggering around the stage and passing out. Was it too much to ask?

Sam Kowalski—who was playing her husband, Lester—was copying the writing techniques into his exercise book. Some of her friends, particularly Maddie, had started teasing her about Sam. He was a good actor, probably the second best in the class. The main problem was that he hung out with the footy boys who always came in stinking of sweat after lunch. Some of their answers in class made her feel embarrassed for them. Sam had started growing a blond moustache in recent weeks. She wondered, at odd moments, when he was going to shave the thing off.

Another aeroplane glided past. She'd never been on one. It was difficult to fit long trips in around her dad's schedule. Marilyn used to fly overseas every winter. Her aunt had always had an exotic, almost tropical aura. No one else Emily knew wore colourful Balinese dresses to the races. When Emily was little, she thought Marilyn was cultured in a way that none of the other local women ever could be and she firmly believed that it was because her aunt got to fly on more aeroplanes. Whenever Marilyn visited them, it was as though everything slowed down and took on a more casual feel.

The first thing Marilyn always did when she visited on Christmas Day, aside from fixing a drink, was walk out to the stables. Sometimes Emily caught her kissing the horses between the eyes and whispering to them. Marilyn had named Jubilee Mile, her dad's most famous racehorse. She used to brag about it every Christmas. A friend of Emily's parents' from the farmers' market once observed that the family all talked about Jubilee Mile as though she was Emily's sister. At the time Emily had thought it was a compliment.

She remembered a party at their house years ago, after Jubilee Mile had run second in the Seymour Cup. Everyone was happy. Even her mum's cheeks were flushed. Late in the evening she'd gone exploring and had found Marilyn trapped underneath her boyfriend Dan in one of the vacant stables. They were both wriggling about and groaning. Marilyn had a strange, wide-mouthed expression. When she finally noticed Emily, she yelled, 'Dearie me!' and jumped up, brushing the straw off her dress. Dan gave Emily a piggyback ride back to the house, breaking into a gallop and whinnying.

Dan was always so much fun to be around. He was ten years younger than Marilyn, but they seemed to be 'on the same wavelength', as her mum put it. He had hair down to his shoulders, he played guitar and he knew all kinds of card tricks. Emily always made sure there was a deck handy come Christmas Day. It was sad the year Dan didn't show up to do card tricks. Since then, Marilyn had brought a number of men along who all made Emily feel uncomfortable in a similar way. One of them said he made his living betting on the greyhounds. Another borrowed Marilyn's car one morning and never returned it.

Last year's man—a chef at the RSL—dropped by late one night in tears, asking her parents for money.

It was funny now, thinking back on it all. When Emily was younger, she had wanted to wear the same lipstick as her aunt and she had wanted to laugh her aunt's happy laugh because it was so contagious. She even tried to hold her plastic cup with the same cocked wrist when she was drinking lemonade at her friends' birthday parties. Marilyn knew how to have fun. Not like Emily's parents. Their lives were bound by rules, many of them way too strict, and they always seemed to want to limit the amount of fun everyone was having.

But now, after seeing Marilyn's half-closed eye when she'd answered the front door the night before, and overhearing her parents consoling Marilyn in their bedroom, Emily pitied her aunt for the first time.

■

As soon as the lunch bell rang, Emily hurried out to the football oval. It was soaked and covered in stud marks. Her shoes quickly became caked with mud. She wasn't sure where she was going, but she wasn't in the mood for the gossip of the canteen. It always stank of dim sims anyway. She turned around to make sure no one was watching then made her way down a slope behind the cricket nets. At the bottom of the slope, she found a trail that looked like it led into the heart of the nature reserve.

She'd never followed it before. There was a rehearsal straight after school so this was the last chance she'd get to spend any time alone. Her chest felt lighter already.

There were tyre marks all along the trail. Brown water trickled beneath the embankments and kangaroo droppings were scattered on the wet grass. After walking for ten minutes, Emily rounded a bend that opened out onto a lake where a rusty dinghy was moored. Beside the boat was a sign reading: PRIVATE PROPERTY NO FISHING NO SWIMMING. The reflection of the eucalypts on the water's surface reminded her of the Impressionist paintings they'd studied in art history.

'Greetings, Ms Corby,' said a familiar voice, startling her.

She glanced to the right and saw a man sitting on a big rock no more than ten metres from her. It was Mr Whitlock, the most popular teacher at school. He was wearing a grey duffle coat and holding a purple book.

'I wasn't aware that students were permitted to leave the school grounds at lunch,' he said, raising his eyebrows. 'I trust you have a note from your parents.'

'No, sorry.' She considered using Marilyn as an excuse, but decided it might make her seem weak. 'Are you going to tell anyone?'

He massaged his sharp chin and smiled cryptically. 'Should I?'

'No, sir.'

'Seeing as we're no longer on campus, you can probably call me Jonathan.'

She felt herself smile. 'Okay, Jonathan.'

'Much better.' He removed a bookmark from his coat pocket and slotted it into the book.

'What are you reading?' asked Emily.

'Nothing exciting, I'm afraid. It's just a style guide. We teachers don't get much time for what I like to call pleasure reading.'

'We don't either with all the homework you guys give us.'

'I can assure you we're only retaliating,' he said, raising both hands as though he was surrendering.

'So are you going to dob me in or not?' she asked, surprising herself with how unafraid she sounded.

He smiled again and laid the book down on the rock. She'd never had him as a teacher. When he took spare periods, all of the students seemed to be on familiar, kind of friendly terms with him. She'd never seen him lose his temper, or even come close.

'So, the play,' he said. 'How are the lines coming along?'

'Fine. I've known them for weeks.'

'Any nerves?'

'No, I don't really get that way.'

'Excellent.'

Emily wished that Marilyn could bring a man like Mr Whitlock to their house next Christmas Day.

'Are you coming to see it?' she asked.

He nodded.

'What night?' She hated herself for sounding so obvious.

'Tomorrow. I've been looking forward to it actually, which is a bit of a rarity when it comes to school productions. Many moons ago I studied the novel. Back before penny-farthings became obsolete.' He chuckled to himself. 'Let the record show, that was a joke.'

Emily tried to laugh, but instead produced a fake, high-pitched sound that was unlike any other she'd ever heard herself make.

'I wanted to play Dolly Pickles,' she said. 'But they made me play Oriel.'

'What's wrong with Oriel? She's probably the most important character in the book, or play, rather.'

'She's too serious.'

'Who cares? Oriel's the unsung hero. Without her, the whole house would fall apart.'

'You think?'

'Trust me, it's a great role. And I'm sure you'll nail it. You were great in *Antigone* last year.'

A strange thrill raced through Emily's body when she realised that he was aware of her theatrical past. In the seconds that followed, it became more of a tingle.

'Do you mind if I sit down for a minute?' she asked.

'Be my guest.'

She sat on the edge of the rock, centimetres away from the style guide. Mr Whitlock glanced at his watch and started absently inspecting a patch of moss with his fingers. He was an odd man, she thought. The only thing she could remember hearing about him was that he used to teach in the city.

'You're obviously very serious about acting,' he said. 'Is it something you see yourself pursuing?'

'I'm not really sure. I think maybe I'd rather be a vet.'

'Excellent,' he said, nodding. 'And why is that?'

'Whenever the vet comes to the stables, she seems so at peace around the horses and the horses look more peaceful around her. I kind of envy that.' Emily stopped and dug at some moss herself. 'I don't really know if that's a good reason to want to do something.'

'Of course it's a good reason,' he said, looking at her so hard that something seemed to plummet inside her chest. 'What was it Churchill once said? "The outside of a horse is good for the inside of a man."'

She tried to laugh without making that weird, high-pitched sound again.

'Has your dad trained many winners lately?'

'One of his horses ran a place up at Kilmore on the weekend, but other than that, he hasn't had much luck. His best horse strained a ligament in his foreleg last start.'

'Is that serious?'

'It can be.'

'Well, it sounds like you know the drill, Emily.'

Another tingle spread through her body when he said her name. The left side of her chest was starting to ache. Maybe this was what having a stroke felt like.

'Is everything okay?' he asked.

'Yeah, fine.' She tried to breathe slowly through her nose, which usually worked when she was about to go on stage.

'Well, don't worry, I haven't taken to bludgeoning students in the woods just yet.' He smiled self-deprecatingly. 'Let the record show, that was also a joke.'

'Sorry,' said Emily. She was desperate to keep talking to him, but she didn't know what else to say. She felt her nails dig into the moss again, finding the grit of earth under the chunk she was pulling up.

'It's a lovely spot, isn't it?' he said, shifting his gaze from her and looking out over the lake. 'I read here every Wednesday and Friday at lunchtime. It's a great way to escape the feigned niceties of a staffroom.'

He looked at his watch again and began fastening the toggles on his duffle coat. 'Now if you'll excuse me, I have the delightful year tens.'

He reached for the style guide. As he was gathering it, his knuckles brushed against her stocking. His touch seemed to linger briefly on her right thigh. The tingling was becoming unbearable.

'Thanks for the chat,' he said, patting the dirt off his navy trousers. 'Not that it ever took place.'

He raised his finger to his lips then set off along the trail, taking measured strides to avoid the puddles. He started whistling just before he turned the bend. Emily realised that she was trembling all over.

■

Marilyn barely touched her plate of lasagne at dinner, but then Emily couldn't remember her ever having much of an appetite. At least she seemed calm, even when she caught Emily looking at her eye. It was starting to turn purple. Most of the talk was about the play. Emily was already over it. The way the other kids were all such drama queens, taking themselves so seriously, like they expected some casting agent from the city to travel all the way to their hick school and sign them up.

Her thoughts slid to Mr Whitlock's touch. His soft knuckles on her thigh. There was no way it was an accident. She'd think about it later when she was alone in bed. She felt too guilty letting herself get excited now, when her family were all sitting around the table, so sad and serious. But she couldn't help thinking about it. Even a boring family dinner felt somehow different;

heightened and strange, like she'd spent the first sixteen years of her life on autopilot, waiting for something like this to happen.

Her dad went to bed after eating a whole packet of chocolate-covered macadamias. Marilyn didn't tease him for hitting the hay early like she usually did at Christmas. Emily ran through her scenes with her mum in front of the fire. Her script was dog-eared and covered in annotations. Marilyn sat on the couch nursing a mug of hot chocolate, watching them and smiling. She was wearing a borrowed woollen jumper that swallowed her whole upper body. Every time Emily got to the end of one of her longer speeches or tirades, Marilyn broke into applause and said, 'Well done, sweetie!'

While Emily was brushing her teeth, Marilyn asked if she'd like to help her with a jigsaw puzzle. The picture on the box was of eight horses crossing a river, with trees, swirling clouds and snowy mountains in the background. It was called 'Last of the Wild Ones'. Most of the pieces were spread out across the kitchen bench top. Marilyn had already started forming the border. They bent over it together, figuring out where the sky and the water pieces fitted in. Emily noticed that Marilyn was having trouble connecting the pieces because her hands were shaking and she realised that she was unused to seeing her aunt without a glass in her hand.

'Does the sound of that fridge ever annoy you?' asked Marilyn. 'It's like there's a boat motor in there or something.'

'I guess I'm just used to it.'

'Do you mind if I turn it off for a couple of minutes?'

'No.'

'Thanks, sweetie; it's giving me a bit of a headache.' Marilyn walked over to the fridge and flicked the switch off at the power point. 'That's better,' she said.

They went on assembling the border pieces in silence. Every so often Marilyn glanced up at a framed picture on the kitchen wall. It was of Emily's dad and his old strapper standing next to Jubilee Mile outside the Seymour Racing Club, smiling broad, contented smiles.

'This is actually fun,' said Marilyn.

'I know,' said Emily. 'It's a great way to keep my mind off the play.' She was dying to get to her room and she felt bad for lying. 'Are you coming tomorrow?'

'Of course, sweetie. I wouldn't miss it for the world.'

Marilyn had missed *Antigone* the year before, even though she'd promised to come.

'Does it hurt?' asked Emily after a while, keeping her eyes glued to the sea of tiny cardboard pieces in front of her.

'No, I can hardly feel it anymore,' said Marilyn. She pressed two fingers against the bruising on her upper cheek. A yellow tinge had started to form around the purple. 'I've got a fractured eye socket. They took an X-ray today. Apparently it's called an orbital fracture.' She gave a small, dry laugh. 'See, I learnt something new.'

Emily couldn't tell whether Marilyn wanted her to laugh too.

'Once the swelling goes down, they're going to make me have surgery. I hate needles, so I'm trying not to think about it.'

'Needles aren't that bad,' said Emily.

'I know, I know, but every time I see one go in on the telly, I have to look away or cover my eyes.' Marilyn shivered and then sighed. 'I look a bit ghastly, don't I?'

They both laughed this time. Emily's mum walked into the kitchen in her dressing gown and glanced at them as she rinsed a mug in the sink. She usually let four or five mugs build up in the bedroom before bothering to wash them.

'Don't stay up too late,' she said to Emily on her way back to the bedroom.

They returned to the jigsaw puzzle and linked up the shallows with the riverbank.

'I miss Dan,' said Emily, surprising herself with her impulsiveness.

'We all do, sweetie,' said Marilyn, leaning in sideways and rubbing her shoulders.

'He was my favourite,' said Emily.

'I know.'

'Why did you break up?'

'I wasn't expecting an interrogation,' said Marilyn wryly. 'Your poor aunt is in a very fragile state.'

'Sorry.'

'No, I'm kidding. I always like talking about Dan. He was such a cutie, wasn't he? I used to call him "cutie pie", but he hated it. I think in the end we just wanted different things, that's all.'

Marilyn started playing with the pile of pieces in front of her. Her hands had finally stopped shaking.

'It doesn't always have to be a big, dramatic ending, even when two people love each other. You'll learn that. Sometimes people just grow apart or want different things, and if you accept it instead of fighting against it the whole way, it isn't always such a horrible thing for everyone.'

Emily didn't really feel like Marilyn was in any position to be giving relationship advice. 'Have you seen him around at all?' she asked.

'No, I haven't seen Dan in years. I know he's got kids now, which is great, because it's what he always wanted.'

Emily found the last piece of the border. 'This morning in class, for some reason I was thinking about the time I busted you and Dan at the stables.'

'Busted us doing what?' asked Marilyn.

'You know, it was after Jubilee Mile's famous race.'

Marilyn squinted with her bruised eye and shook her head.

'I'm pretty sure you guys were in the middle of . . . Hang on, do you really not remember what I'm talking about?' asked Emily.

'I've honestly got no idea, sweetie.'

■

The boys from the junior campus got on the bus at the stop opposite BP. One of them, a scrawny redhead whom the others called Ferret, had lost his ticket. He rustled around in his pockets and in his backpack for change, but he couldn't find any. None of his friends had any change, either. The driver shrugged and grumbled, 'No ticket, no ride.'

'I'll pay you back tomorrow,' pleaded Ferret. His voice still hadn't quite broken. 'Please, I've got a science test first period.'

The driver shook his head.

'I promise I'll pay you.'

'You're making me late,' said the driver, raising his voice. 'It's time to step off the bus now, mate.'

Ferret obeyed. He was left standing on the wet grass in front of the shelter, staring at the bus.

'Sorry, rules are rules,' said the driver, catching Emily's eye in the rear-view mirror.

She knew what he meant. As long as he was behind the wheel, the bus belonged to him and it was his right to decide who got to go on it. For all the things he didn't have a say in, this small bit of power was entirely his, and if he gave in, even just once, the kids would use it against him forever. Not that any of them probably gave him a second thought once they stepped off the bus. The only thing the driver had in his favour, thought Emily, was that unlike Marilyn, he wasn't pretending everything was rosy all the time.

She'd always assumed that people were where they were by choice and that they had got there by going down a carefully considered path. Her parents seemed happy enough with their life, always smelling of hay and grain and selling nuts at the farmers' market every second Sunday. Had they made compromises too? It was frightening to think that adults' lives might be full of mistakes and regrets, and that so many of them might feel unhappy when the lights went out at night. Maybe even Mr Whitlock had dreamt of bigger things than standing in a classroom in his early thirties, being worshipped by small-town students.

She kept replaying his words: 'I read here every Wednesday and Friday at lunchtime.' They had to be an invitation. There was no other reason for him to mention it to her. He knew what he was doing the whole time at the lake and he knew what he was doing to her inside at the moment. He had to feel something too. Why else would he have pressed his finger against his lips before walking away?

She couldn't stop imagining what it would be like if she turned up at the lake tomorrow. He would be sitting on the rock, waiting for her. The intensity of his gaze would make her tingle. He'd crack some self-deprecating jokes to put her at ease. His first touch would be tender, understanding that she was shy and that she hadn't done any of it before. Finally he'd kiss her. The toggles on his duffle coat would press against her chest and his hand would start running up her stockings.

All of a sudden Emily was wrapped up in a big hug. She doubted that the driver approved of Maddie's over-the-top greetings.

'You look like shit,' squealed Maddie.

'Gee, thanks.'

'It's not that bad, you've just kind of got these bags under your eyes.'

Emily had still been lying awake when her dad got up to feed the horses.

'I'm so looking forward to the after-party,' said Maddie, elbowing her in the ribs. 'You'll finally get to see what Sam's bedroom looks like.'

Emily rolled her eyes. 'I bet there's footy posters everywhere.'

'You never know. There might be dirty magazines in his drawers.' Maddie smiled, covering her mouth with her hand to hide her braces.

'Do you think he's going to shave that awful thing on his face off before the play?' asked Emily.

'You're so mean! I think it looks good.'

'Seriously?'

'Yeah, it makes him look rugged, like a woodchopper or something.'

Emily had always played along with such talk because she was scared of the consequences of seeming uninterested. But she now understood how someone's whole mood could depend entirely on their interactions and imagined interactions with just one other person.

'You had Mr Whitlock last year, didn't you?' she asked, as if it was a random passing thought. Even just saying his name gave her a thrill.

Maddie nodded. 'Yeah, we had him for English.'

'What was he like?'

'I don't know, he was okay. Everyone else loved him. He was always crapping on about what book we should read next. It kind of got a bit annoying. Plus he's got a crap sense of humour.'

'What's wrong with his sense of humour?'

'He's one of those people who thinks he's funnier than he is,' said Maddie. 'But none of the jokes he makes are actually funny. I couldn't even figure out when he was joking and when he was being serious.'

Maddie flicked her hair out of her face and it fell back again in exactly the same place. God, she was dumb. She pulled an open packet of salt and vinegar chips out of her backpack and held it out. Emily took a chip, but felt sick once she'd swallowed it.

'Why do you care, anyway?'

Emily shrugged, being careful not to overdo it. 'I'm worried I might get stuck with him next year.'

Maddie smiled and put her hand in front of her mouth. 'I heard he smoked a joint with the year twelves on muck-up day last year,' she said.

'Who told you that?'

'One of my brother's friends. Mr W. busted them smoking behind the footy oval, but he didn't give a shit. Then someone offered him the joint and he took a turn on it.'

■

Emily tried not to blink while Maddie applied her eyeliner. All of the other girls were putting on their own, but Emily had never learnt how to do it. She hated wearing make-up; it made her feel so unnatural. Plus it was a pain in the arse taking it off before bed. But when Maddie finally stepped away and let her look in the mirror, she wasn't quite as put off as usual. Her eyes seemed more defined and she was surprised by how much older she looked. The fact that she looked nothing like Oriel Lamb no longer seemed to matter.

Fifteen minutes before the play was due to start, she peeled back the curtain to take a peek at the audience. The basketball markings were covered by plastic chairs, most of them still empty. She saw Ferret sitting in the front row with his parents, who seemed to confirm that he was the product of inbreeding. Sam Kowalski's dad was sitting alone. The principal was standing near the entrance to the gymnasium, shaking hands. Emily spotted her mum and dad in one of the middle rows, near the emergency exit. Marilyn was sitting on the end of the row, wearing sunglasses.

There was something she loved about the lull when the lights dimmed and everyone—cast, stagehands and audience—realised that a performance was about to begin. She could feel the intensity of the silence and the sense of expectation in the air. The only experience that came close to it was the tension she used to feel as a child when she watched one of her dad's horses entering the mounting yard before a big race. The main difference now was that the outcome was in her hands.

By the time she made her first entrance onto the stage, most of the chairs had been filled. Even though it was a frenzied opening scene—the near drowning of her son Fish—she felt herself drop effortlessly into character. Once she'd blurted out her first maternal cry, thumping her son's waterlogged chest, Oriel Lamb seemed to flow through her. She became this scarred, unrelenting woman. Sleeves rolled up. Fists drawn in to her ribcage. Corns and bunions on her feet. It was a piece of cake. She even found herself prevailing over the comic overacting of the boy playing Fish.

She enjoyed her onstage fights with Sam Kowalski. She channelled her repulsion towards him and his ridiculous moustache to show Oriel's exasperation with her husband. He played off it to perfection, bowing his head at the appropriate moments and protesting pathetically as only Lester could. He even had this weird way of stooping so that he looked timeworn. They reached her favourite scene in the play, when Lester was trying to convince Oriel that their pet pig could talk. Sam delivered his lines with just the right naïve excitement, creating the opening for her to belittle him and milk laughs from the audience.

Then, just as their dialogue was about to reach its climax, she caught sight of Mr Whitlock sitting behind Sam's dad. He appeared to be watching like everyone else in the audience, absorbed in the marital tension, but his eyes were fixed on her. His expression didn't change when her eyes met his. It pierced her concentration, taking her outside of her character and causing her to lose the arc of Oriel's emotions. Sam was in the midst of an uncharacteristically bold protestation, so she had enough time to remember her next line, but she felt the tension and the believability ebb away. She stumbled through the remainder of the scene, trying her best to regain the measure of her character. But she no longer believed it herself.

■

There was something comforting about the foggy windows, the crunching of the gravel underneath the tyres and the puffs of dust in the high beams. The car was nice and toasty. Emily's dad yawned and checked the time on the digital clock. It was already three hours past his bedtime. Marilyn wasn't wearing sunglasses anymore. Emily was looking forward to winding down by working on the jigsaw with her once they got home. Marilyn had already finished the sky and the clouds and was now working her way down from the tips of the mountains.

'You were incredible tonight, sweetie,' Marilyn was saying. 'I was so proud watching you up there.'

'Thanks.'

'How did you even learn to act like that?'

Emily felt herself flushing with pleasure. 'I don't know, I guess it's just practice.'

'You were so convincing. I actually believed you were that grumpy woman.'

'Oriel,' said Emily's mum from the front seat.

'That's the one: Oriel. It felt like you were really her. I can't believe I'm related to someone so talented. I hope you want to be an actress when you grow up.'

'I haven't really decided yet.' Even though Emily's dad had never actually asked whether she wanted to work at the stables when she was older, she was sure that he wanted her to.

'Well, I thought you were the star of the show,' said Marilyn.

'Me too,' said her mum.

'And I think you're going to be a famous actress someday,' added Marilyn. 'If you want to be.'

Emily's dad chuckled.

'What's so funny?' asked Marilyn.

'Nothing,' he said, still chuckling.

Emily ran her fingers along her forehead. The foundation was starting to feel crusty. Had Mr Whitlock liked seeing her with make-up on? She recalled the intensity of his gaze in the audience. There was no doubt anymore that he wanted her to meet him at the lake.

'What's the name of that boy you were married to in the play?' asked Marilyn.

'Sam,' said Emily, already knowing where it was going.

'I sensed definite chemistry.'

Emily shook her head. 'He's not my type.'

'I don't know about that,' said Marilyn. 'I think he's going to be very handsome.'

'Why don't you date him then?'

'There's no need to get defensive, sweetie.'

'Leave her alone,' said Emily's mum.

They were almost home. She stared at the foggy rows of the winery, hoping that she'd finally be able to get some sleep tonight. Marilyn was doodling on the window, her finger trembling. Emily's dad slowed the car as they approached the pine tree plantation.

'That could be a good one,' he said, pointing to a small tree on the side of the road.

'You just concentrate on driving,' said her mum, slapping him on the shoulder.

Two weeks before Christmas every year, he'd take the HiLux out at night and saw down a pine tree from the side of the road. Afterwards they'd all decorate it in front of the fireplace. He always boasted that he was saving the family forty dollars on a tree, but Emily suspected that he'd saw one down every year even if it didn't save them money.

'All I'm saying is, it's got potential,' said her dad, not daring to glance sideways. 'You've just got to picture it in another four or five months.'

'You're on your last warning,' said her mum.

Even though it was too dark to see her expression, Emily knew her mum was smiling.

■

Her drama teacher kept the class back after the lunch bell to run through the schedule for the bump-out. Then the other kids kept asking annoying questions about the after-party. Sam assured everyone that his dad wouldn't care if there was drinking. Emily kept glancing at the clock on the classroom wall. He'd probably be at the lake already. She felt like she was going to throw up.

When the class was dismissed thirteen minutes late, she told Maddie she was busting and made a run for it.

She was panting by the time she emerged from the underpass. Two buses were parked at the terminus. There was an interschool football match going on. Boys with square shoulders were shouting and whistles were being blown. Some of the girls from her year were barracking from the hill overlooking the oval. They were so pathetic. She tried to sneak behind the cricket nets without anyone noticing her. The grey-bearded driver from the last three mornings was standing in the shade, leaning against the nets and reading a newspaper. He glanced up as she walked towards him.

She climbed down the slope that led to the nature trail, being careful not to slip on the grass, before breaking into a jog again. The sun was poking through the tall trees and most of the mud on the trail had already dried out and hardened. It was difficult running in her school shoes because they kept losing traction on the dirt. Her heart was racing. Perspiration streamed down her forehead. She was starting to get a stitch. There was barely any saliva left in her mouth. She hoped her breath didn't smell. She reached into her blazer pocket and took out a packet of chewing gum that she'd bought from the canteen at recess.

Every stride was bringing her closer to him. It was probably best this way, meeting him head on, so she could finally stop thinking about it. He'd know what to do. She was happy to abandon the play, if he wanted. She didn't care where they had to go or what they had to give up to get there. She could keep any secret. But could the bus driver? He definitely knew something was going on and for some reason that made her feel guilty. Was it too late to turn back? They hadn't broken any rules yet. But it felt like something had already begun, something serious, and she'd regret it forever if she didn't go through with it.

Life wasn't meant for regrets. There was no use ending up like Marilyn, pretending to be happy with the hand life had dealt her. What was she doing right now? Probably sitting at the kitchen bench with a midday soap playing in the background, working away at the jigsaw and waiting for the swelling to go down. They'd found the mountains and the trees the night before. All that remained now was to find the rest of the water and to work their way into the bodies of the wild horses.

Marilyn could finish the puzzle by herself, and Emily didn't care if she never saw another one of her aunt's colourful outfits. The fascinator she wore to Jubilee Mile's last race was so over-the-top. The race had been up in Wangaratta and Jubilee Mile was taking on a galloper from the city over twelve hundred metres. She set the pace for most of the race, just like she was supposed to. Usually once she hit the front in the straight, no horse could get near her. But something went wrong. The jockey knew it straight away. He tried to relax her. She faded and finished near the back of the field.

The vet was already at the stalls by the time the family got there. No one knew what to say. Then Jubilee Mile's hind legs suddenly gave way, then her forelegs, and she was down, the big muscly shining weight of her still and heavy on the ground. Emily's dad was panicking in a way she'd never seen before. It didn't suit him. As the stewards started arriving, Marilyn had picked Emily up and carried her away. She struggled in her aunt's arms, just wanting to see it all for herself, hearing the murmur spreading through the grandstand, that lull just before something big and important happens.

No one was holding her back anymore. She could imagine what it felt like to be a horse, drawing oxygen into her giant lungs and galloping towards the winning post. Her stitch had miraculously vanished. She was so close now. He was so close. She couldn't quite believe it was happening. She rounded the final bend and there he was, just as she'd imagined, sitting on the rock. Everything was so still. He smiled knowingly and put down the style guide, as though nothing out of the ordinary was about to take place.

HINTERLAND

'Good luck,' said Sonny, shielding his eyes from the glare and squinting through the open window of the yellow kombi.

He was left standing on the side of the old Pacific Highway, looking out over the lush, subtropical terrain of the Brunswick Valley. He slung his backpack over his left shoulder and set off.

By the time he'd walked all the way to Uncle Tom's Pies, he wasn't hungry anymore. Two petrol bowsers stood out the front of the roadside bakery. He'd always loved the smell of petrol. It reminded him of being out on the boat with his dad at Blackwall Reach, fishing for mulloway, when he was supposed to be sitting in a cramped classroom.

He turned left and followed a sealed road in the direction of town. He stuck up his thumb out of habit, not caring whether anyone pulled over. It was around three o'clock in the afternoon by his reckoning. He was getting better at guessing the time. A fortnight ago he had donated his watch to a young boy in a roadhouse on the Eyre Highway. He already missed the dry heat of the desert.

No cars passed by in either direction for the best part of half an hour. He lowered his right arm and climbed a steep hill, enjoying the strain on his calves, which were bronze, taut and hairless. Even though it wasn't particularly hot, the back of his shirt was sopping. At the top of the hill he caught sight of a mountain that soared above the rainforest, piercing a bed of white clouds and dwarfing the township of Mullumbimby.

Vast rows of banana plantations stretched across the surrounding hillsides. He didn't eat bananas anymore. The price had quadrupled since the cyclone up north the previous summer. He was happy to go without small luxuries if it kept him on the road a little longer. There'd have to be a job soon, though. He just hadn't found the right place.

On the outskirts of town he passed a group of stilted houses with tiled roofs. The houses were painted aqua, lime and peach. It reminded him of a big fruit salad. The front porches were cluttered with old mattresses, camping chairs, pot plants and deflated footballs. Most people's lives were one big mess, he was starting to realise, and maybe he was lucky to be rid of it all, not tied down in any way, even if things did get a bit lonely from time to time.

He stopped at an op shop that was inside a Seventh-day Adventist church. It was closed. Clothes were scattered across the car park and a stack of crockery was leaning against an overflowing charity bin. He sorted through the clothes and picked out a long-sleeved shirt that he could see himself wearing to a job interview.

He crossed the railway tracks. Thistles protruded through the planks and the platform was deserted. He remembered what the widow who'd given him the lift had told him when he asked about work in the local area. Three years ago trains had stopped running between Casino and Murwillumbah, she'd said, as though the town had already been written off the map.

Even though she was a local, she didn't seem to care. She didn't seem to care about much. Her husband had suffered a brain haemorrhage the day before his forty-second birthday. Sonny had no idea what any of the medical terminology meant, in spite of the widow's lengthy explanations. He'd just sat there next to her in the kombi and nodded, feeling the engine eating up the kilometres that he no longer had to walk.

■

The publican at the Middle Pub was standing behind the main bar, polishing a rack of pint glasses. An elderly man with a grey

222

crew cut was slouched over the bar talking to him. Every so often he glanced over his shoulder in Sonny's direction. Sonny didn't think the publican needed any help behind the bar and there wasn't much else going on in town from what he could see out the window.

Sonny finished his beer and walked over. He decided to wait until there was a pause in the conversation before ordering another beer.

'It's easy for you,' the elderly man was saying to the publican. 'You've got a great commodity.'

The publican made eye contact with Sonny, but before he could order, the elderly man laid a hand on Sonny's forearm. His grip was surprisingly strong. 'Guess how long I've been selling fuel,' he said.

'Leave him alone, Turbo!' said the publican.

'He doesn't mind,' said Turbo, maintaining his grip. 'You don't mind, do you?'

Sonny shrugged.

'See, he doesn't mind. Go on, guess how long.'

'You don't have to guess,' said the publican dryly. He slung a damp tea towel over his shoulder and slotted the rack of pint glasses underneath the bar.

'No, no, he wants to have a guess,' said Turbo. 'I can feel it in my bones.'

'I've got no idea,' said Sonny.

Turbo took a gulp of beer and grimaced. There was something about the grimace that reminded Sonny of his dad and all his dad's old friends.

'Go on, have a guess. Pick a number.'

'I can't think of a number.'

'Jesus almighty, they breed them dim these days. I'm worried this young fellow won't even land a job stacking shelves at Woolies.' Turbo produced a spurt of laughter. 'Alright, alright, I'll tell you. Twenty-one years. Twenty-one years of sweat. But we all know the drill. The big boys come to town and the rest of us just get swept away.' He finally released Sonny's arm.

'Do you know of any jobs going at Woolies?' asked Sonny, trying to be proactive.

Both Turbo and the publican looked at him like he'd said something shameful. He was starting to feel like this wasn't the town for him and that the bright lights of Tweed Heads might be a better bet.

He bought a schooner and returned to his stool by the window. The sun had finally breached the low-lying clouds and was gushing over the palm trees. Rainbow lorikeets were chattering away in the branches. Aside from three dodgy-looking kids lingering outside a pizzeria, the main street was dead. There'd even been more action in Bangalow.

Sonny spotted a crumpled form guide on the floorboards near his feet. There was only one race remaining at Randwick, but there was a night meet at Ascot in Perth. He'd grown up in a flat a few kilometres from the track. He used to love it when his dad took him down to the track to watch visiting horses labour when they hit the uphill straight. They'd laugh like it was just the two of them in on the joke. But even then when he could see his dad's yellow teeth, a part of Sonny still knew that his childhood wasn't going quite how it was supposed to.

He read the form guide and marked the horses he liked with a red pen. When he'd finished he stood up and walked into the small sports bar, but there was still ten minutes until the final race at Randwick. It was probably a good thing that he was trying to watch his money. He knew that once he placed that first bet, no matter how good he was feeling about it, his life might as well be over.

He went and had a good look at the slot machines. He understood how it could all become comforting, like a home away from home. That patterned carpet, the glowing screens and the high-pitched noises from the machines. Sonny's dad once drunkenly told him that the only two spots where time never dragged were out on the water and playing the slots at the casino.

He joined a small congregation in the sports bar to watch the final race at Randwick. It was a Group 3 handicap. His money would have been on an outsider to run a place. He rated the jockey. Besides, there was no value in betting on favourites. The horse missed the start, but ran gallantly through the middle stretch. It got boxed in on the rail when the field turned for home. The jockey led the horse wide in an attempt to gain a run at the post, but it was no use. The horse ran a narrow seventh. Sonny decided it probably wasn't a bad sign.

■

A three-piece band was tuning up on a small stage in the corner of the main bar, where tables and chairs had been shifted out of the way to make a temporary dance floor. Sonny ordered a beer from the publican's wife, a heavy woman who looked like she could hold her own against anyone in the bar if push came to shove. He couldn't wait to get that next schooner into his body. He was feeling a bit of a buzz coming on, which was a rare thing, probably because his dad let him try it out on the boat when he was only nine years old. There'd been a few chunks in the water afterwards, but it had all been smooth sailing after that.

He settled on a stool at the bar and faced the stage. The band began their set with a slow blues song before shifting into an upbeat country number. Some devoted locals took to the dance floor. They seemed to be hearing notes that escaped Sonny's ears, but then he didn't really know much about music. He would have liked to play an instrument, and to be up on stage, but he doubted that he'd be able to hold a rhythm.

The guitarist broke into a solo and an emaciated man with a long rat's tail performed a strange dance, his legs quivering uncontrollably. He opened his mouth and wailed over the top of the music. No one seemed to mind. He was missing most of his teeth, which allowed him to unfurl his tongue and ripple it in time with the music.

A young Aboriginal man shuffled his way from the dance floor to the bar and took the stool next to Sonny. 'Woo-ee!' he said, wiping his brow.

Sonny took a long drink from his beer and continued to watch the man with the rat's tail, who was now crooning to a nearby woman. He wasn't getting much enthusiasm back.

'Bullfrog will go all night, don't you worry about that,' said the Aboriginal man, releasing several short breaths.

'I'm sure he will.'

'The name's Roy,' said the young man, offering his damp palm.

Sonny introduced himself and Roy repeated his name out loud. Sonny often found that people enjoyed saying his name. He wasn't sure why.

Roy ordered a shot of tequila. 'I live upstairs,' he said, pointing at the ceiling. 'I'm the only permanent lodger. There was a bloke named Sid and his daughter, but they shot through last month. We'd been working at a site in town.' He surveyed the dance floor.

'What kind of site?' asked Sonny, hoping that something might come his way out of it.

'An unpopular one, if you follow my meaning. We started the job six months late, lots of protesting and angry letters. I try to stay out of it. The way I see it, none of it's on me.' Roy knocked back his shot of tequila.

'Word is we'll be finishing up soon. Not fussed either way. This is a nice place,' he said, looking Sonny in the eye, his hair glistening with gel. 'Sure as hell nicer than where I come from.'

Roy's face was round and cushioned and he had more wrinkles than Sonny, even though he didn't look much older than eighteen.

'My girlfriend's staying with me tonight,' said Roy. He pointed at a slim girl with long limbs on the dance floor. 'She goes to school in Lismore. Every Saturday night she comes to stay with me, lies to her parents, says she's sleeping at one of her friends' houses. We don't get much sleeping done.' He nudged Sonny. 'Truth is, we're not supposed to see each other anymore.'

'What's her name?'

'Danielle.'

Sonny finished his beer and ordered two more schooners.

'Thanks, mate,' said Roy.

They watched Danielle sway to the music. No one else in the bar was swaying. She kept her eyes closed the whole time. Every so often she ran her fingers through her hair, allowing it to fall over her exposed shoulders.

'If you don't mind my saying, she's very beautiful.'

'Music to my ears,' said Roy, slapping Sonny on the back. 'I'm hoping to put a ring on her finger sometime soon. I've just got to figure out the right way to make it happen. Hopefully I can put away enough money here to buy a nice big diamond ring, something she'll remember forever. Don't want her telling her friends I skimped on the ring.'

'What about her parents?'

'I might just have to shoot them.' Roy slapped Sonny on the back again.

'Good luck with that,' said Sonny, hoping Roy knew he was only joking.

He recognised the next song. It was a fast cover of a famous Slim Dusty ballad.

Roy drained the rest of his beer. 'I love this one,' he said, rising from his stool. 'Listen, do you want to dance with me and Danielle?'

'No thanks.'

Sonny watched Roy shuffle back over to Danielle. Bullfrog's legs were quivering again. Roy approached Danielle from behind and put his hands over her eyes. She surrendered to his touch, allowing herself to sink into his outstretched arms.

■

At the beginning of the band's second set, Sonny bought a six-pack over the counter and walked upstairs. He found the communal kitchen at the end of the hallway. Turbo was slumped on a couch in front of the television, snoring. The south-east Queensland derby was on and the crowd was going berserk over something that'd just happened. Sonny watched for the next few minutes, hoping for fireworks, but everything started to die down, so he retreated down the hallway.

His room, which was directly above the main bar, had a double bed, a bedside table, a desk and a big wardrobe. He lay on the bed. The furnishings were much nicer than he was used to. If only there was a bit of work going around, he could have lodged there with Roy and made a good fist of it. His arms felt itchy. He'd suffered countless mosquito bites since setting out along the east coast. Back home the mosquitoes had no interest in his blood, but that was about the only reason he could think of to ever go back.

The music from downstairs was making the bedframe vibrate. It sounded so repetitive, probably repetitive enough for him to fall asleep, if he wanted. But it was too early. Then it would just be another wasted night. He cracked the first of his beers and drank it lying in bed. It felt like the kind of thing that his dad would have done, getting half-cut in a strange room in a strange town, dwelling on everything that hadn't quite worked out in his favour.

He stood up and walked over to the mirror above the desk. On looks alone, he was almost an interesting person. Bloodshot eyes, long straight nose and a fluffy beard that was slowly starting to get some coverage up around his cheekbones. His thin chestnut-coloured hair was beginning to look unruly around his ears, which he liked, but he could already see how his hairline was going to recede in the middle, just like his dad's had over the years, and how he'd eventually have to accept it and shave all his hair off.

He moved to a table on the balcony right outside his room and started playing a game of solitaire, but he soon lost interest and opened his second beer. He looked out over a deserted intersection in the centre of town and then into the darkness where he knew the mountains and the valleys were. His eyes were drawn to the orange hue of a telephone booth on the opposite side of the street. A young woman was holding the receiver and chatting away. Sonny wished he was on the other end of the line, telling the girl how much he missed her, not that he could even see her face properly.

■

'Sonny-boy!' said Roy, appearing on the balcony hand-in-hand with Danielle, his black hair pasted across his forehead. As Roy was getting two chairs from a nearby table, Sonny looked down and saw Bullfrog being helped across the intersection by two men. His legs weren't quivering anymore.

'Been wondering where you got to,' said Roy. 'Still owe you a beer by my count. Maybe this'll even things up a bit.' He reached into his shirt pocket and produced a joint. 'Any objections?'

Sonny shook his head.

Roy lit the joint, inhaling several times in quick succession before passing it to Danielle. He only let her inhale twice. Sonny puffed on the joint three times and handed it back to Roy. He'd never really smoked much because his dad didn't like to mix it with the drink.

Danielle shifted onto Roy's knee, put her head on his shoulder and wrapped her arms around his thick neck. Sonny realised that Roy had a wonderful neck for a football player. Danielle closed her eyes and Roy started stroking her fine hair.

'Got to wake up at five in the morning so we can climb Mount Warning,' said Roy.

'Sounds exciting,' said Sonny, having the strange sense that he was suddenly talking outside of himself.

'Yes indeed, we want to be the first people on the mainland to see the sun come up,' said Roy, still holding in his smoke. 'Nice and romantic.'

He kissed Danielle's hair. Sonny enjoyed seeing the soft swelling of her ribs, but he stopped looking because he didn't want to upset Roy, even though Roy hadn't shown any hint of an aggressive streak.

'Are you sure you'll be able to get up on time?' asked Sonny, wanting to keep the conversation going.

'The way things are stacking up, I might need to push on through to the morning,' said Roy. 'Maybe you can help me out on that front.' He grinned and stubbed out the joint in the ashtray. 'Naturally you're welcome to join us.'

'Why not, I guess,' said Sonny, feeling good about things.

'Always happy to share the good times among friends,' said Roy, grinning. 'Hopefully there's plenty more of them to come.'

They fell silent.

Sonny drained the rest of his beer and placed the empty bottle on the table, next to the deck of cards. There was no longer any commotion coming from downstairs. He'd lost track of the time. It was much harder to tell the time at night, especially once alcohol entered the equation. He wondered whether they should be concerned about keeping the noise down. He didn't want to wake the publican, or his wife.

'What's on your mind, stranger?' asked Roy.

'Nothing, I was just wondering if the pub's closed.'

'Yes indeed,' said Roy, grinning again. 'And you know what they say, don't you, Sonny-boy?'

'No,' said Sonny, confused.

Roy started singing the Slim Dusty ballad from earlier, closing his eyes and tipping up his mouth to face the roof.

Sonny's dad's drinking friends had belted out the exact same song at his funeral, as though it was supposed to be some big sentimental moment they were all sharing.

'Hate' was the word that suddenly came to mind. He hated everything about his dad. All those fishing trips, pretending it was a father–son thing. They never did any bonding. He was just stealing Sonny away from the real world, taking him out on the water for company. He didn't even make a big deal of it when Sonny caught his first flounder and had so much excitement stuck in his body that he felt like he was going to explode.

Roy was up to the chorus now.

It had been hell sitting there in his Salvation Army suit, watching those red-cheeked men belt it out. Sure, they were all honouring him in their sad old ways, the seven men who'd bothered to show up, but there was one way Sonny could tell the truth and that was by watching their faces. No one shed a single tear the whole funeral.

'You with me, Sonny?' asked Roy, waving his hand from across the table.

'Sorry, what?'

'Looked like you were drifting off someplace.'

'I was, but thanks for bringing me back.'

'No sweat,' said Roy. He pulled out another joint and lit it.

'I was just saying, seems you know all about me, but if we're going to be mates, I'm going to have to know something about you,' said Roy. 'So what's your story?'

'My story,' said Sonny, playing with the unruly hair around his ears. 'I don't think I have one yet.'

THE GIFT
OF
LIFE

My childhood friend Leo Rosenbloom lived in a Californian bungalow. It was a two-minute run from my house. His mother, Jeannie, worked the evening shift at Piedimonte's. She was a large woman who used to dye her hair auburn every month, but not before her grey roots would emerge.

Leo's father, Abe, was born in Russia. I couldn't pronounce the name of his home city. He was unemployed. He used to lie in bed most of the day, facing the wall, listening to a silver transmitter that let out lots of beeps. He didn't like being interrupted while he was listening to the transmitter, but it all just sounded like static and beeps to me.

The main thing I didn't understand about the Rosenblooms was why they always left their front door open during the day. It even stayed open when no one was home. I sometimes walked past their house on weekends and imagined that the whole place was yawning. I preferred to knock when I visited, even though it seemed pointless waiting at an open door.

They were robbed twice when Leo and I were in grade three. Abe and Jeannie were both home the second time. Jeannie was cooking and Abe was lying in bed, listening to the transmitter. The robbers took a wooden stringed instrument—which Leo called a *gusli*—from his bedroom. He had to stop having lessons. After the second robbery the Rosenblooms finally started closing their front door.

Leo was almost as obsessed with cricket as I was. We created a makeshift pitch in his front yard by placing a rubbish bin at the head of the concrete pathway. We glued one- and two-cent pieces along the path to make sure there was enough variation in bounce. Jeannie didn't like the look of the coins on the concrete, but because they had no other visitors, she never bothered to remove them.

It took us a whole afternoon to come up with the rules. There were all the normal modes of dismissal, plus automatic wicket-keeper. Any ball that hit the side of the picket fence was worth two runs. Any ball that reached the front of the fence was a four. Any ball that bounced on the road on the full was a six. And any ball that landed in a neighbour's yard was six and out (plus the batsman had to jump the fence and get the tennis ball).

Our games were played over two innings, which meant that we each got to bat ten times in a row (barring declarations). We swapped hands to impersonate the cricketers we idolised. I loved pretending to be Clive Lloyd, the giant West Indian captain known as 'Big Cat'. It took weeks of practice to learn how to copy Lloyd's relaxed, bottom hand batting technique. I hated getting dismissed cheaply when I was being Big Cat.

Our childhood seemed like a never-ending battle against the fading daylight. Neither of us ever wanted to stop playing cricket. We often ended up playing in complete darkness to reach the conclusion of a match. No one ever called us inside.

When it wasn't cricket season, we played downball with Alexander Kostopoulos. His parents owned the milk bar on the corner of Leo's street. We played on a sloping quadrangle outside his parents' garage door. Occasionally Alexander's father would roll up the door and interrupt our games to speak sternly with his son in Greek.

Alexander played games differently to us. He didn't have any sports heroes to pretend to be. There was something funny and aggressive about his movements. We both enjoyed competing against him. He always beat us at downball. Yet, unlike the other kids at school, he never teased us about it.

The kids at school called him 'Zorba' and tried to get him to dance by clapping their hands faster and faster. I was never sure who coined the nickname or what it actually meant. He didn't particularly like it. I sometimes got the feeling that he wanted to use his knuckles in the schoolyard but had already learnt the reasons why he shouldn't give in to those impulses.

Alexander stole lollies from the milk bar. He gave them to us in white paper bags, which he plucked from the inside pockets of his bomber jacket. The bags were chock-full of bananas, raspberries, teeth, liquorice, big bosses, bullets, fags, sherbet bombs, musk sticks and stale clinkers. Much to our bemusement, he never seemed interested in eating the lollies himself.

He said he was just like the famous mobster Al Capone, smuggling alcohol in America during the Prohibition years. Neither Leo nor I had heard of Capone or Prohibition, but we were happy to play along.

On sunny afternoons Alexander often insisted that we lie in the street and pretend to smoke big bosses. He would blow out a thick cloud of imaginary smoke whenever a beautiful woman walked past. Every woman looked beautiful to me. In spite of the funny looks he usually got, he assured us that the women had been impressed.

At the beginning of our ninth summer, a nasty piece of graffiti appeared on the side of the milk bar. It was about Alexander's mother. A fortnight later the milk bar changed hands and he stopped coming to school. The hardest part for Leo and me was the realisation that we would have to start paying for lollies again.

■

Alexander's departure seemed to release something in Leo and me. We became more adventurous, crossing main roads, running through sprinklers and pooling our pocket money to buy fish and chips. We passed many hot afternoons on the summer holidays in Curtain Square, eating off fat-soaked butcher's paper. We also took to playing chicken with the number 96 tram. Leo always lasted a little longer than me before dodging the oncoming carriages.

Abe's beard grew long and grey. He reminded me of a famous bushranger we'd learnt about in school. He no longer bothered to greet me when I visited their house. I barely saw Jeannie. She was working extra shifts at Piedimonte's on weekends so that she could buy a new *gusli* for Leo. I didn't like spending time inside their house because of the nonstop static coming from the silver transmitter.

We started meeting outside the Nunquam sweets factory instead. I loved the minty smell that surrounded it. We sometimes took turns trying to stand on each other's shoulders by the window in the hope of glimpsing the sweets being made (we'd heard that the factory used a hundred-year-old peppermint lozenge machine). We both wanted to work there when we were older because we imagined that it would allow us to eat as many Nice Mints as possible.

While we were walking past the Nunquam factory one afternoon, a stranger started leaping around on the footpath in front of us. He was making a funny noise that sounded like a horse's whinnying.

'You bloody ripper!' he shouted. He held two fifty-dollar notes in the air. It was more money than I had seen outside of a television screen.

'I've been looking for this money for over an hour!' he said, panting and smiling. 'It must have fallen out of my pocket.' He let out another whinnying noise. 'Once I saw you two kids I looked down and there it was, just lying on the footpath.'

He shook our hands. 'I can't thank you two enough,' he said, bowing. He was balding on top of his head, but he had furry hair all around his ears.

'That's okay,' said Leo.

'There must be something I can do,' said the stranger. He paused. 'How about I shout you both an ice-cream to say thank you? It's the least I can do. You've saved me a hundred dollars.'

It was a boiling afternoon. The grass in Curtain Square was yellow. The offer of a free ice-cream seemed too good to refuse. Yet somehow I had the feeling that the offer was Leo's to consider.

'We could go to Yumbo's,' said the stranger. He held the money in front of our eyes.

'Say yes,' I whispered to Leo.

'See, your friend wants to go,' said the stranger, looking at Leo. 'Come on, what do you say, sport?'

Leo twisted his lips. I didn't know what that look meant. The only time I had seen a similar look on his face was while he was waiting for Abe to slowly finish his food at the dinner table.

'No, we better not,' said Leo.

I was shocked that he had refused such a kind offer. I couldn't help but resent him for it.

'Come on now, I couldn't live with myself if I didn't do something nice for you kids,' said the stranger. 'I've been on my hands and knees for an hour.' He crouched on the footpath, showing us how he'd been searching for the money. There was a hole in the knee of his trousers.

'I'm not really hungry,' said Leo.

'You sure?' The stranger shifted his eyes to me. His head was shining with sweat.

'I think we better go home,' said Leo.

'You can have as many flavours as you want,' said the stranger, sounding more like a kid than us.

'No,' said Leo. 'But thanks.'

He started walking away. The stranger continued to crouch on the footpath. He ran his hand through the furry hair around his ears and dropped it to the concrete. His pose didn't look quite right outside the Nunquam factory. I wondered whether the minty smell ever made the workers feel sick.

I caught up with Leo as he was crossing the tram tracks. We kicked an empty Coke bottle along the footpath, but we didn't talk. When we reached his front gate he said, 'It wasn't our money.'

'I know,' I said.

He dragged his family's rubbish bin across the pathway and lined it up in its proper place. He handed me his heavily taped bat. There was still some string left on the handle. He reached his bowling mark and started polishing the tennis ball on his shorts. He practised his action several times. It was identical to that of the great Pakistani all-rounder Imran Khan.

I stared beyond his arm at the fruit trees, the terrace houses and the purple sky and I hoped that darkness would never come.

ACKNOWLEDGEMENTS

Thank you to Nam Le, for breaking the levee with his boat, and to Allen & Unwin, for taking a risk on me. I'll never forget it.

For their sharp eyes, my thanks to Cate Kennedy, Ali Lavau, Clara Finlay and Tim Fry, who have all made these stories indisputably better.

For feeding me, driving me and letting me be driven, my thanks to everyone I'm lucky enough to call a friend.

My heartfelt thanks to the lovely Laura, for eating greasy food in bed with me and taking on an extra special needs student.

Finally, my thanks to Anne, Lauren and the silliest man alive.